A Twisted Kind of Love

By Ashley Burton

Murder with
Pleasure
Ashley Burton

This book contains dark subject matter. It is intended to be read by adults 18+!

I dedicate this book to my husband and bestie.

Thank you both for believing in me!

Without you two, I would've given up a long time ago.

Love you both!

Prologue

Present Day...

Mason,

Looking back on us, I see that I should've never let our relationship escalate as quickly as it did. I should've set up boundaries early on. God, what have I done to us? It's my fault. I take full responsibility. I just never realized that we were headed down the path we were and going to fall so fast and deep.

I'm so sorry that this all happened. I just want you to know that,no matter what happens, I'll always love you. You'll always hold a very special place in my heart. Please don't try to find me. I'm doing what is best for the both of us. We are too volatile together. Together, I fear we'll lose ourselves and become this massive tornado destroying everything in our path.

Before you do anything that you'll later regret, hear my words. Let me go… Just let me go, Mason.

Love Always,

Reagan

Let her go? What the fuck? That's like asking me to rip my heart out of my fucking chest and keep on living. I close my eyes and take some deep breaths. I wasn't ever going to let her just fucking walk away from me, from us. We were meant for each other!

Chapter One

Mason

Summer of 2007

My bedroom vibrated from the bass of my stereo blasting some rap song. I'd randomly hit a station that sounded decent, earlier. Sweat poured down my body as I pounded the punching bag hanging in the corner. I was trying to blow off some steam. My old man was always on my ass or my mom's. Although, I really didn't give a fuck when he was on her's. She was a timid little mouse of a woman.

I often wondered if she even birthed me. She never looked at me with any emotion. She was like a fucking statue. The only time she ever muttered a word was when she'd had a little too much brandy. That's when the fireworks went off. A few slaps from my father and she was back to being the timid little mouse.

Dear old dad was in his study with his buddies right now. They were in a 'meeting' about the stock market. Stock market, my ass. They were each taking turns fucking that luscious blonde they'd walked in with. I felt my cock stir thinking about her. She had those plump lips, gorgeous eyes, and some big titties.

I pounded the bag harder. I could call Mallory and she'd come over to help ease my discomfort. I was tired of her pussy, though. We'd all had it.

"Mason, son. Get in here!" My father's voice boomed down the hallway. Fuck! I gave one more good punch before stomping to the door. I didn't bother grabbing a shirt. Hell, maybe big tits would see my abs and decide to give me a go.

Without knocking to announce my arrival, I swung the door to my father's study open and walked into a cluster fuck. The blonde was on her knees sucking off Dave, one of my father's friends. My father, Charles Winston, owner of a large upscale jewelry chain was fucking her in the ass. In the corner was Frank, another of my father's associates, jacking off.

With a guttural groan, my father pulled out and came all over the blonde's ass. Staggering to his feet, he took a deep breath before grabbing the blonde's hair. "Clean my dick off, bitch." she licked her lips while staring up at him. When she had him inside her mouth, he gagged her with his dick while slapping her in the back of the head. "That's it, take it all like the dirty little whore you are."

This all seemed to get Dave all hot and bothered because he ejaculated all over the floor. What the fuck? My father groaned again before blowing another load in the chic's mouth. With a sigh, he finally turned his attention to me.

"Mason, son. Would you show Candace out?" What? The bitch could show herself out? I wasn't the fucking butler.

My father didn't seem to like what he read on my face. "Wipe the fucking frown off your face. This is grade A pussy I'm throwing your way. Enjoy it."

She got off her knees and came over to rub her hand down my stomach, before cupping my dick. Yeah, bitch, it was limp from watching the old man gang bang that just happened. There was still some of my old man's jizz on her lip. "Clean up. Then, I'll fuck you." Turning around, I stalked out of the room and back into mine. I opened the drawer of my night stand, grabbing a condom.

I heard her shut the door and turned towards her. "On your knees." I dropped my gym shorts and stepped out of them. Her eyes widened when she saw the size of my dick. That's right, honey. I'm hung like a fucking mule. She licked her lips but her eyes showed her apprehension. I fisted her hair and shoved her head towards my dick.

Thrusting into her mouth, I hit the back of her throat and wasn't even halfway in. She gagged, her eyes watered. I held her down on it for a few minutes before letting her free. I stroke my dick while I make the bitch suck my balls.

"Now, go bend over the bed." Her ass was in the air. I had to give the old man props. He was right. She had a fucking beautiful pink pussy. I bent down and stared at it. Opening the lips, rubbing my fingers over her clit. She moaned and pushed against my fingers. Getting her juices all over my fingers, I rubbed them up and down from her ass back to her pussy.

Grabbing the condom, I ripped the wrapper open with my teeth. "You ready to be fucked, Candace?" She threw me a sultry look over her shoulder. I saw my tie hanging on my bedpost and grabbed it. I decided to have a little fun. I looped it over her head and tightened it on her throat. I tugged on it until she made a choking sound. My dick pulsed in response. I felt cum leak from the tip.

I slapped her ass and told her to flip over. Her large breasts bounced when she laid on her back. I licked my lips. They weren't fake. I slapped the both of them a few times, turning them red. She groaned and bit her bottom lip.

I pinched both of her large nipples, tightening on them until she yelped. Without warning, I thrust into her wet channel. Unfortunately, she wasn't too tight for me since she'd been fucked a few times just minutes before. I loved the pain I caused women on our initial fuck. I ached to make them bleed a little for me.

I thrust a few more times, getting the condom nice and lubricated from her juices. Grabbing her legs together, I threw them over my shoulder and push inside her ass. It on the other hand was a little harder to slip into. My father wasn't as endowed as I was. She whimpered when I bottomed out. The heat and tightness of her little ass made me groan. She tried to pull back but stopped when I slapped her face.

A drop of blood left her lip and made me harder. Fear lit her eyes and awakened the beast within me. Pulling out, I plunged back inside. Harder and harder each time. She began to cry. I grabbed the tie when I got tired of her wailing, tightening it on her throat. Spreading her legs, so I could lay on her and watch the life leave her eyes. Her face began to turn red, then a beautiful purple. Her fingers grabbed for the tie, but I grasped both of her wrists with my hand and held her still. Her body thrashed against me, but I kept pistoning my hips in and out of her ass.

The light began to leave her eyes, her body shuddered before growing completely still. Right before my climax hit, I pulled out and jerked the condom off. Stroking myself, I ejaculated all over those gorgeous tits. Loosening the tie, I admired the bruised necklace it left.

Turning my back to the beautiful whore, I headed to my bathroom and hit the shower. The hot water cascaded down my back and helped calm down my inner beast. Closing my eyes, I replayed those seconds before the life had left her eyes. My dick got hard again. I wanted to fuck her again. Too bad, her body was probably already getting cold. Grabbing the body wash, I poured a generous amount in my head and stroked my dick. Using the images of her tits bouncing and the blood dripping down her lip, I came again. Thick ropes of cum hit the shower walls.

Finally, feeling sated, I grabbed a towel and dried off. Wrapping it around my waist, I headed to my father's study. Pausing to listen to the men inside laugh. "Wonder if Mason busted a nut before he even got inside her."

A dark chuckle left my lips as I pushed the door open. "Well boys, she's well and properly fucked. Why don't you come admire my handy work?" They all grinned before rising from their seats. They were all back dressed in their suits. I let them lead the way to my room. All three of them circled my bed staring down at the whore with a mixture of horror, disbelief, and disgust.

"What the fuck have you done?" Frank's voice was low. There was an edge of caution to his questioning, though. He was scared of me. That was good.

"I fucked her." Dropping the towel, I went to the dresser and pulled on some boxers. I headed to my closet and grabbed jeans and a tshirt. When I was dressed, I headed downstairs leaving them with the chore of disposing of the whore. I glanced back once, my father was at the top of the stairs, staring at me like he'd never seen me before.

I heard my mother weeping in the formal living room and shook my head. The woman had known they were fucking that slut upstairs and didn't give a shit. Not that she could've stopped them anyway. I often wondered why my parents had even married. They seemed to hate each other.

Turning back to the old man, "you knew what the fuck was going to happen when you gave me the bitch. Now, you can clean up the fucking mess."

Fall 2012

Courtney was bent over my bed taking my dick up her ass like a pro. Her moans spurring me on. She had a hand between her legs, stroking her pussy to bring on her orgasm. We called her Courtney Cat because she sprayed like a fucking cat when she came. I felt it hit my balls before she let out a scream of ecstasy.

Slapping her ass, I pulled out of her and took off my condom. She knew the drill. Turning around, she clamped her lips around my dick and sucked. Her hand cupped my balls, squeezing them. Deep throating me as much as she could handle, she stroked as she sucked. I closed my eyes, thinking how pretty she would look beneath me, dead.

Jets of cum left me, filling her mouth. She swallowed every drop, moaning. She tried to raise up and wrap her arms around me. Not going to happen, bitch. I grabbed her cheeks with my right hand and squeezed. “You know the drill, Courtney. Now, go shower so we can get to school.”

My bedroom door swung open, my father standing in the doorway taking in the scene. Courtney sat up thrusting her small, perky breasts out. “Hey, Mr. Winston.” His eyes raked down her body, his hunger shown through. Hell, I didn’t care what the fuck they did. I was hitting the shower. I had football practice and couldn’t miss school.

I shut the bathroom door behind me, listening to the seduction going on in my room. I heard my father’s heavy step head in the direction of my bed. A zipper sounded and his groans echoed. She wasn’t making a sound, so she must be sucking him off. I chuckled thinking of all my cum she’d just swallowed.

Shaking my head, I let the shower wash her off of me. I hated school but I loved football. The physical violence of it helped me feed my dark side. I still had slip ups here and there. Fortunately for me, my father’s good friend Frank owned a very lucrative funeral home. I’d padded his wallet with cash over the years for all the cremations he’d done in exchange. I was smart, though. I only unleashed the beast with whores. They had no family. And, no one ever looked for them.

Give them a hit of ecstasy and they did whatever the fuck you wanted.

Chapter Two

Reagan

I laid in my bed staring up at the water stained ceiling. I was dressed and ready for my first day at Wedgemont High. I hated starting a new school. I couldn't count how many times I'd had to over the years. It fucking sucked. All the whispers, stares, and hostility. All the fucking clicks constantly judging.

My mother's latest conquest was currently in the kitchen yelling at her about burning his breakfast. He was the reason I was remaining in my room until the last possible second. The sound of flesh striking flesh had me jumping up and running down the tiny hallway of the trailer we had rented two days ago. The bastard had my mom on the kitchen floor punching her face. I jumped on his back, tackling him to the floor. Jumping up before he could get his hands on me, I gave a swift kick to his middle.

His sharp intake of breath told me I'd hit my mark. I delivered another kick before stomping on the hand he'd used to hit my mother. Mom was rolling around on the floor, holding her face. "Nice one you picked this time. I'm going to school."

With that, I grabbed my backpack from the chair and strolled out. Slamming the door behind me, I began my walk to school. Glancing down at my outfit, I couldn't stop my grin. I was always referred to as white trash, slut, the girl from the wrong side of the tracks, trouble, and so on. After a while, the insults started rolling right off my back. I began to embrace them. There was no use in letting them know that they'd got to me with a few of those names.

I couldn't help the life I had been born into. I was none of those names. ALthough, I loved having fun with the idiots that threw those insults my way. I loved dressing the part. It was fun watching the jealousy light up in those mean girl's eyes when their boyfriends drooled over me. I wasn't going to lie, I have a nice body. I'm five foot six with long legs, c cup breasts, small waist, and a nice booty.

This morning I had chosen ripped jeans, knee high black boots, and a black tank top that was little low cut. If I lifted my arms the little devil tattoo on my side peeked out. I smiled when I thought about what the tattoo stood for, my first and only love.

I pulled the front door of the school open and took a deep breath. The pity looks would start from the office personnel because I was by myself without a parent. I rolled my eyes and braced myself.

The secretary was pretty generic. She was a tired, overweight, middle aged woman who was on the grumpy side. After I filled out the forms, she printed out and handed me my schedule.

"Oh wait. Mason, dear, could you show Reagan where her first class is? She's a newbie." She had a big smile for whoever the Mason was. I turned and felt my lungs fail me.

Mason had sandy colored hair that was styled messy on top of his head. His green eyes seemed to see right through to my soul. When I finally got myself to move away from his eyes and focus on the rest of him, my heart started pounding. He had great skin, full lips, and a muscular body. I found myself wanting to rub my hand down his chest and breath him in to see what he smelled like.

Shaking my head, I pushed my shoulders back and went to move around him. I didn't have time for high school boys. I had a boyfriend, kind of.

"Hey, hold on there." His voice was deep and seemed to make butterflies take over my stomach. His hand landed on my shoulder, pulling me back. I swear I felt like I'd been scalded. Jerking away, I met his gaze. Hunger and something dark lurked in his eyes. This guy was hiding something. But, what?

"Let me see your schedule, so I can at least point you in the right direction." He took it from my hand and studied it before smiling. "Well, we have all the same classes but two. Come on." He lifted my backpack off my shoulder and carried it on his thick forearm.

“I’m perfectly capable of carrying my stuff.” I tried to pull it back but he lifted it over his head, still smiling.

He didn’t say anything just kept walking. I grabbed at his arm, it was pure muscle. He came to a sudden stop when I touched him, which caused me to crash into his back. He stiffened against me. His scent filled my nose. It was pure male with a hint of cologne. I caught myself before I sniffed him. God, what was wrong with me?

I caught him looking at me over his shoulder. Pure lust filled his gaze. I licked my lips and ran my hand down his back.

“While I’m enjoying your hands all over me, it would probably be a good idea to stop while I still have control of myself.” His voice was even deeper and scratchy. I was affecting him just as much as he was me.

Part of me wanted to see how far I could go before his control snapped. Would he throw me over his shoulder and take me outside to have his way with me? Would he slam me against the lockers and take me right here? There was a darkness inside him that beckoned me. At the same time, that darkness scared me. It was still there, lurking in his eyes, almost taunting me.

He let out a sigh, before turning around to face me. His hand reached up and cupped my face. His thumb stroked my bottom lip, causing me to shiver. My nipples hardened beneath my tank, drawing his eyes. Yep, that's right, I wasn't wearing a bra. Slut 101 will teach you to always go commando. His tongue licked his lower lip as his eyes raked me up and down.

Dropping his hand from my face, he closed his eyes and took a deep breath. "I can't miss class because I have football practice after school. So, I'm going to need you to behave and follow me to class."

I let him get a few steps ahead of me before following him to class. Everyone got quiet when we entered class, all eyes staring. I heard one girl whisper, "who the fuck does she think she is letting Mason carry her shit?" Uh oh, already getting catty and they don't even know my name. I smirked at the blonde and her little friend. Cheerleaders. They were both decked out in their uniforms.

Mason said he was on the football team. So, they probably had fucked him at some point. Everyone knew the cheerleaders were nothing but the football team's on personal fuck toys. Rolling my eyes, I turned my attention to the teacher. I let out a sigh when I saw the teacher checking me out, not even trying to hide his interest.

"Okay class. We have a new student joining us. Her name is Reagan Smith. Let's all make her feel welcome. Just take a seat wherever."

Mason handed me my backpack and I headed for the back row of desks. Picking the one on the end, I slid into my seat and set my backpack on the floor beside me. I looked up when I felt someone beside me. Mason slid into the desk right next to me. I knew it wasn't his normal spot when everyone, including the teacher, was staring at us. I propped my feet on the chair in front of me and crossed my arms over my chest.

I stared straight ahead at the chalkboard, ignoring all of them. I cut my eyes to the side and saw Mason staring at me, he winked. I couldn't hold back the smile that grew into a low giggle. He was going to be trouble.

Class was boring as always and seemed to take hours to get through. I made it through another class before it was finally lunch time. I was starving but had no money, so I made my way to sit outside and enjoy the sunshine. Mason grabbed my arm before I touched the door to go outside. "Where are you going?" His eyes stole my breath again.

"Outside, I'm not really hungry." I winked at him and went to head outside again. He refused to let go, though. Giving him my attention again, he nudged his head toward the cafeteria.

"Come on. You can eat with me." His voice was so commanding. Panic filled me when I thought about how I couldn't pay for food. Taking a breath, I decided to stick with my not being hungry. I'd sit with him if he insisted.

Of course, eyes followed us as we went through the cafeteria. We got in line and he grabbed a tray. I just stuck behind him. He grabbed two slices of pizza, a container of french fries, two sodas, and two cookies. He really must be hungry. Then, again, looking at his hunk of a body, it must take a lot of fuel to keep him going.

He picked an empty table and sat down. I went to walk around the other side, but he grabbed my hand again. Pulling me down, I sat right next to him. He pushed a slice of pizza, a cookie, and a soda my way. He put the fries between us and winked.

"I told you that I wasn't hungry, Mason." I was dying to eat but I had pride.

He shrugged his shoulders. "I don't like to eat alone." I smiled and shook my head. I wasn't a wasteful person, so I took a bite of the pizza and had to stop myself from moaning. It tasted so good. I hadn't eaten in almost a day. Food was scarce at our place and usually whatever man mom was doing at the time laid claim to it all. So, I was stuck sneaking to eat whenever I could.

I loved my mom. She just had her priorities all fucked up.

I had the pizza inhaled in no time. I popped the top on the soda and took a sip to wash it all down. Grabbing the cookie, I had it gone in three bites. Mason nudged the fries in my direction. When I looked at his face, he wasn't paying me any attention. He was still working on his pizza. Without thought, I began munching down on the fries. I had them eat in a few minutes. They were really good.

I grabbed a napkin and wiped my hands and mouth. I looked at Mason and he was grinning. “So, where do you want to grab dinner later?”

I blushed. “Thank you for lunch, Mason.” He winked at me and stared into my eyes. God, he was so intense.

“You’re welcome, Reagan. I was serious when I asked you out for dinner.” His voice was so deep. I felt my nipples harden, which of course his eyes went straight to. He licked his lower lip.

Deciding to play with fire, I leaned in and ran my fingers along his thick forearms. I ran my tongue along my bottom lip. “What would you like to eat for dinner?”

His eyes went straight to mine. “You.”

His voice was so husky. That one word went straight to my pussy. I felt it pulse and get wet. I fidgeted in my seat, squeezing my thighs together to get relief. He smirked as if he knew what was wrong.

I winked at him and gathered my trash. I walked to the trashcan and threw my stuff away. I headed towards the doors to spend the rest of my free time outside. He followed me. Right as I stepped out, he grabbed me and led me behind the cypress trees that lined the walkway. My back hit the brick wall and his arms trapped me in. His scent hit me and took over my senses.

I looked into his beautiful green eyes and felt myself struggling to breath. His eyes were full of hunger and that darkness that always seemed to lurk there.

"I want you, Reagan. I want you to be mine and only mine." He stroked my face. His mouth was inches from mine. "Do you understand?" Before I could answer, his mouth crashed against mine. His tongue breached my lips and claimed my mouth. I moaned and sagged against him. My arms wrapped around his neck and my body pushed against his.

Our tongues dueled against each other. His erection pushed against my stomach. He felt massive. I rubbed my tits against him, seeking relief. His hand came down and squeezed one, groaning in my mouth when he rubbed my nipple.

I pulled back when I felt myself ready to throw all caution to the wind and fuck him right here. Despite the rumors that seemed to follow me everywhere I went, I was still a virgin. Not that I was completely innocent. I was told I gave great head.

Dropping to my knees, I pulled down Mason's zipper. I fumbled with his boxers, struggling to release his massive dick from the opening. When I finally got him free, I felt myself swallow. God, he was fucking huge. I'd never seen a dick that size. I honestly, didn't think such a thing was possible.

Licking my lips, I stared up at him, he seemed surprised that I was daring to do such a thing. I gripped his dick in my hand, squeezing. His answering groan, encouraged me. I opened my mouth and took what I could inside.

I couldn't fit all of him in my mouth. It just wasn't possible. But, oh he tasted so good. I moaned when I tasted the precum that seeped out of the head of his dick. Pulling back I swirled my tongue all around the crown of his cock. I looked up at him and saw the raw hunger on his face.

I pumped his cock up and down with my hand as I worked my mouth up and down as well. His hips began to thrust in and out of my mouth. His hands fisted my hair as he held me still so he could take over. I heard him groan before I felt his cum shoot all in my mouth. I struggled to swallow all of it. It was so thick and so much of it, but I got it all down. His salty taste made my pussy pulse.

I closed my eyes when I thought about what the fuck I had just done. I'd just sucked a guy's dick that I hadn't even known a full day. I had just lived up to my nickname, whore.

Taking a deep breath, I looked up at Mason to judge his reaction. He was still staring at me with raw need on his face. God, this guy could be the death of me. His fingers trailed my face, his index finger rubbed along my bottom lip.

"This mouth belongs to me now, Reagan." He pulled me up and assaulted my mouth with his. I moaned when he squeezed my breast with one hand and pushed his other hand down my jeans. His eyes widened when he noticed there was no panties to act as a barrier between him and my pussy.

His fingers slid between the lips of my pussy and stroked my clit. His mouth closed over mine to capture my moans. Fuck, this felt so good and so bad at the same time. When I felt his fingers inching towards my entrance, I grabbed his arm to stop him. Pulling away from his mouth, I shook my head. “Just my clit.” My voice came out raspy.

He looked confused but moved back to my clit. He was stroking circles around and around it, before lightly pinching it. God, he was making me crazy. I was strung so tight, I knew I was going to blow at any minute. He was nipping his way up and down my neck, his other hand was torturing my nipples.

The door slammed near us, making me jump. Mason pulled away and straightened my tank top. I watched him put his dick away, amazed that he was hard again. I shut my eyes and tried to regain my composure. I was so fucking horny and really needed that orgasm to take the edge off.

Mason leaned back into me, capturing my mouth with his. The kiss was slow, deliberate, and seemed to claim my soul. He pulled away slowly, brushing his thumb along my bottom lip. “We’ll finish this later. I’m going to taste every inch of your delicious body.” His voice sent a shiver through me. My pussy clenched and I had to close my eyes. What the fuck was wrong with me? I’d never been so amped up over a guy. Well, I take that back. Devil, my kind of boyfriend, could get me worked up. I hadn’t seen him in a long time, though. I, honestly, didn’t know what our relationship status was. But, I had known that when I got involved with him.

The truth was, though, that I’d made out with guys and given Devil blowjobs. And, now, Mason... But, I’d never fucked anybody. I knew after what had just occurred between the two of us that Mason would expect us to fuck later. So, I needed to come clean with him. He’d probably end up pissed and call me a cocktease.

“Mason, I need to be straight with you.” My voice came out low, almost a whisper. I was nervous. I really liked him and I didn’t want to fuck up. I’d already fucked up by sucking him off after just meeting him. He was eyeing me with curiosity and caution.

"I'm a virgin. I know, you're thinking how can a girl that just sucked my dick after knowing me a few hours be a virgin. But, guess what? That's me. And, I swear I'm not a whore who goes around giving out blowjobs. You're the second dick I've ever had in my mouth, I swear. I don't even know why I'm telling you all this. Okay, I'm going to just stop talking now."

His expression was giving nothing away. Great, I'd seriously fucked all this up with my blabbering.

He nodded at me and seemed to be searching my eyes for something. I just didn't know what. He leaned in and kissed my forehead. His nose rubbed down the side of my face and nuzzled my ear. "Who did the other dick belong to?" That question shocked the hell out of me.

"Nobody you know." My heart was pounding out of my chest. Why the fuck did he care?

Mason got even closer in my face. I was breathing the air that he was releasing. His smell was intoxicating. His eyes were probing mine as if he could suck all the answers from my soul. "Who did the other dick belong to, Reagan?" His voice was low with a hint of menace.

A shiver ran up my spine. “Devil.” My voice was barely a whisper.

“Devil?” He gave me a quizzical look, but still intense.

“He’s my kind of boyfriend.” I knew that confession would not go over well.

“Your kind of boyfriend. What the fuck is a kind of boyfriend? And if you have a boyfriend, what the fuck are you doing on my dick? I’m not going to fucking share you, Reagan.” His fist hit the brick wall behind me, a vein was pulsing in his forehead and he looked ready to explode.

“He and I aren’t exactly official. We’ve hardly even seen each other. He’s always busy with his band and club. And, I’m always at the mercy of fate, it seems. I think we’ve spent a total of a month or two together this past year. I’ve never been his top priority.” My voice is shaky. I don’t know why, because I’ve only known him not even a day. I just really like him. Obviously, since I just sucked his dick and swallowed his cum. God, I’m such a slut. I can’t help it, though. There’s just something about him that draws me in.

Mason has closed his eyes and seems to be concentrating on breathing through his nose. I decide to pull a chic move. I rub my hand down his chest to his abs. My fingers tease the waistband of his jeans. “Mason, really, it's nothing serious. We just kind of liked each other and he’s always said I was his girl.” I sigh when his eyes meet mine, searching. “I really like you. I know we’ve only just met, but I’m really into you.”

He closes his eyes again before closing in on my mouth. His tongue thrusts past my lips and claims me. There’s no back and forth. He takes complete control, conquering me, marking me, making me his. It’s so alpha male. I love every second.

When I moan, he pulls back. His breathing is ragged and his pupils are dilated. God, I want him to be my first. I feel like he would take complete control of my body and leave me a quivering puddle of need. Then again, the size of his dick makes me want to run for the hills.

“Ride home with me after practice, Reagan. I promise, I’ll make you forget anyone before me.” His voice is so full of yearning that my heart cracks a bit. I find myself nodding before I catch myself.

He nods and his eyes seem to light up. “Tell me your address and I’ll pick you up.”

There’s no way in hell that is happening. “How about I meet you somewhere? What time is your practice over?” He frowns at me and seems to be trying to figure me out. Good luck with that buddy. I smirk at him.

“We’re done around five thirty. If you want you can meet me here or I can pick you up anywhere that’s convenient for you.” I nod.

“I’ll be here, waiting. Which vehicle is yours?”

Pushing back from the wall, he studies me for a second. “I drive a blacked out Ford Raptor. You can’t miss it.” He tugs the waistband of my jeans, pulling me to him. Placing a light kiss on my lips, nose, and forehead he throws his arm over my shoulders, steering me towards the doors.

Chapter Three

Mason

God, this girl was driving me insane. I couldn't believe she'd fucking sucked me off during lunch. I'd never felt so out of control before. There was something about her that was getting in my blood. Fuck. She was so hot. That thick auburn hair, whiskey colored eyes, and fucking stacked body.

Shaking my head, I focused on practice. I couldn't let her distract me here. Coach would have my ass. This was my outlet for the built up violence inside me. Tackling, hitting, and just letting it all out helped me control the beast that lurked within. I'd been dying to make Mallory bleed for the past few months, but drilling her in the ass had seemed to be taking the edge off.

The size of my dick had been helping in that department. I always stretched the whores to their max and it always seemed to cause a tad of destruction. They were all well worn, but not by guys with my size equipment. Although, being stretched out helped them accommodate my size.

A sense of pride always filled me when some girl's eyes got big as the eyed my monster. They were used to small or average dudes. They'd never fucked a guy with an almost eleven inch dick. But, it wasn't even the length, which was well above average. The girth of my cock was also impressive. I seen the guy's in the locker room eyeing me with envy. They always tried to hide their dicks. I usually smirk at them. I know what I'm working with.

"Alright, fellas! Good practice. Hit the showers!" The coach's voice bellowed around us. Unsnapping my chin strap, I pulled my helmet from my head. I flipped my hair to the side, sweat flying. Letting out a deep breath, I found myself grinning. I was about to see my girl.

"The fuck you grinning at, Mason?" Austin's voice sounded beside me. I threw him a sideways glance. I didn't like the fucker. He was a sneaky little bastard. Always trailing me at parties, lurking in the shadows. Sweeping in to get my sloppy seconds, like he could shine in my light.

"Wouldn't you like to know." Entering the locker room, I swiped a towel from the shelf and started stripping out of my practice jersey and pads. Grabbing my body wash from my bag, I headed to the showers.

Not giving a shit about my nudity, I showered out in the open. I wasn't one of those pussy boys who had to hide in a shower stall. I rushed through my wash routine, ready to see Reagan. I had to keep my thoughts clean, though. I couldn't be getting a boner in front of the guys. They might get the wrong idea and think I'm gay.

Wrapping a towel around my waist, I went to my bag and got my clean clothes out. When I was dressed, I hollered bye to the other guys and left the locker room. The walk to the parking lot was a rushed one. My smile turned into a full out grin when I spotted those long auburn tresses blowing in the wind. God, I wanted to be balls deep inside her.

She looked up at me and smiled. I felt my heart skip a beat staring at her breathtaking beauty. She began fidgeting as I stared at her. I chuckled. So, she was nervous around me, after having my dick down her throat.

I clicked my key fob to unlock my truck. “Your chariot awaits, my lady.” I opened the passenger side door and she hopped in. Her ass looked great in her jeans. I shut the door and ran around to the driver’s side. Hopping in, I started the truck. “You can listen to whatever you want on the radio.” I glanced at her, she was looking at the inside of the truck.

“You have a really nice truck, Mason.” She leaned forward and searched through my programmed stations until she found something she liked. It was rock, so I was good with it.

I hit the gas and we were headed out of the parking lot. I drove us to the nearest drive thru and ordered some burgers. I knew after the whole lunch experience that she wasn’t likely to tell me what she wanted to eat.

When they handed me the bag, I passed it to her. “Just hand me my burger and the other one is for you.” I grabbed the drinks they passed through the window, putting one in my cup holder and one in hers.

As I was driving away, I saw her reach towards me. I smiled when I saw that she had pushed my wrapper halfway down my burger. She was too sweet. I took a huge bite and glanced towards her from the corner of my eye. She was trying to eat normally, but I noticed she was taking huge bites and closing her eyes, as if to savor the flavor.

I needed to remember to grab her food every fucking time that I did. Obviously, she wasn't getting to eat when she needed to. I was halfway through my burger when I saw her put her empty wrapper in the bag. Damn. Maybe I should've ordered her two.

I had finished my burger and tossed my wrapper in the bag by the time we arrived at my house. I noticed Reagan's eyes were the size of saucers as she took in the size of the place. Yes, dear old dad had to show off his money. We really didn't need a house this size, his ego did.

She got out of the truck after I did, following close behind me. Opening the door, I spotted mom in the living room she used to entertain. She was almost three sheets to the wind by the looks of it. She was sprawled out on her white couch, her silk blouse all wrinkled, and one of her heels had slipped off her foot. It would be quite the spectacle when she decided to get up and fix herself another drink.

Reagan had paused and was glancing towards my mother. I just shook my head and motioned for her to follow me up the stairs. We reached the top and was heading to my room when the door to Dad's study opened. He stepped out and froze when he saw us. His eyes went straight to Reagan. I noticed his face paled and his eyes widened. What the fuck? I looked back towards her and saw her smirk.

"How do you two know each other?" I kept my voice level even though I wanted to scream. I didn't want Reagan to have any fucking ties to my father.

"Son, do you realize who you have brought into my house? She belongs to the son of the local MC's president! You've got to get her the fuck out of here! I can't have them coming here!" A vein pulsed in his forehead and his face had turned red and blotchy.

I glanced at Reagan again and she was grinning like a cat that ate the canary. She'd said that she had a kind of boyfriend, whatever the fuck that was. Was it this biker prick?

"What the fuck is he talking about?" My voice was calm despite the jealousy boiling inside of me.

She looked at me and I saw the guilt lurking there. My heart sank and I, actually, felt sick. What the fuck? I never lost my cool over some chic. And, I hadn't even fucked this one. God, I was turning into a fucking pussy.

"Look, I told you about Devil. We were hanging out one night in the MC's stripclub. This joker came in there and tried to grab me, thinking I was one of the girls working there. Devil and a few of the boys got in his face, telling him he needed to treat me with respect. He got all pissy saying that 'all the bitches in here have a price tag'. Well, this one doesn't. He was drunk and acting like a douchebag. They threw him out on his ass. And, if I remember correctly he's not allowed back in there." Her eyes had an evil gleam to them as she looked straight into my father's eyes.

HIs face was turning red again. “Look you little bitch, I don’t know what the fuck you’re doing here or who the fuck you think you are, but you can get the fuck out!” He went to grab her arm, but I blocked him. I gave his chest a push to put some distance between him and my girl.

“You don’t touch her.” My voice was low but the threat was there. He heard it. The color left his face.

“Don’t do this, Mason. You don’t know what you’re getting yourself into, son.” His voice shook.

“I really don’t give a fuck.” WIth that I turned my back on him. I put my hand on Reagan’s hip and led her inside my room. She glanced around taking in my posters and possessions sitting around. Her eyes stopped on my messy bed before she looked back at me. Her hand seemed to shake as she pushed her hair behind her ear. Her tongue came out and moistened her bottom lip. My cock got instantly hard. This girl was going to be the death of me.

Without thought, I grabbed her and pushed her against the wall. My arm went between her legs, my hand used the wall for balance as I lifted her off the ground so that we were eye level. “Now, be straight with me before this goes any further. Are you and this Devil guy still an item? Or are you going to be my girl?”

Her eyes filled with lust and I saw her nipples harden beneath the tank she wore.

“I’m all yours.” Her voice was raspy. My mouth

slammed against hers, my tongue pillaged her mouth.

My cock felt like it was going to bust the seam of zipper. Jesus, I was ready to be balls deep in her. But, I needed to pace myself. She claimed she was a virgin. I’d rip her apart if I fucked her like I wanted to.

I heard her answering moan as our tongues mated and dualed for dominance. I almost chuckled at the thought of her thinking she could ever dominate me. My cock loved the thought of her riding me, though. Images of her eyes watering while she was choking on my dick almost made me lose my load in my jeans. I didn’t think the denim fabric could stretch anymore to accommodate my hard on. God, my dick needed freedom.

With my free hand, I undid the button and released the zipper. Pushing down on my boxers, my cock sprang free. It bobbed up and down seeking that sweet spot. Reagan's hands fisted in my hair as she strained to rub her tits against me. God, those luscious tits. Grabbing her ass with both hands, I pulled her from against the wall and headed towards my bed. Our mouths never broke contact. My heart was hammering inside my chest.

She had me so worked up, I felt like a fucking virgin about to get his dick wet. I threw her on the bed and watched her bounce. Her hooded eyes looked up at me full of lust. I pulled my shirt over my head, toed off my shoes, lost my jeans, socks, and boxers. Her eyes widened as she got another look at the monster between my legs.

Without pausing to give her time to change her mind, I pulled her tank over head. Those big, beautiful tits bounced as they gained freedom. Before worrying with the removal of her jeans, I had to have them in my mouth. My hands found both the beautiful globes, pushing them together. I tongued the left nipple before sucking the right nipple into my mouth. Reagan threw her head back and groaned.

My balls tightened at the sound of her throaty moan. God, I needed to fuck her. I needed to fuck her hard. I straddled her waist, getting on my knees. I pushed my dick between her full tits. A growl left my throat at the erotic sight. “Spit on it.” My voice was deeper than usual.

She looked down at my dick, licking her lips. Her lips pursed before she spit. It dripped down to the head and ran down my shaft. She did it again and it landed on her tits. I pushed them tighter together against my cock and began to push in and out of them. She moaned again and I felt her squeezing her thighs together beneath me.

I bet she was fucking soaked. Pulling away from her, I bent down and thrust my tongue between her lips again. My hands fumbled with her jeans. When I felt the button and zipper give way, I pulled my mouth away and watched as I pulled her jeans down her long legs. She was fucking commando underneath. No fucking panties hindered me from seeing her bare pink pussy glistening, practically begging to be fucked.

I gripped her thighs, shoving them apart as I bent down and blew air on her wet folds. She writhed back and forth, seeking friction. I kissed her swollen pussy lips, parting her folds with my index finger and thumb so I could see that beautiful clit.

"Mmmm, you look so delicious, baby." She whimpered as I ran my tongue up and down her pussy lips. When I circled her clit, she moaned. Her nails raked my scalp and pushed against my head to keep me there. I chuckled and worked her with my tongue. I circled her tight hole, her juices all over my tongue. I went back up to her sweet clit as I eased my middle finger inside her.

She was so fucking tight. I worked in and out as my tongue flicked and taunted her clit. I felt her tightening on my finger so I eased another one inside her, stretching her out. She tensed up, trying to pull away but I kept her there, fucking her with my fingers. When she began to relax, I pulsed my fingers against her g-spot and thought she was going to shoot off the bed. I looked up at her while sucking on her clit, her eyes were wild and lost in ecstasy.

I felt her coming and pulled my fingers, watching as that sweet pussy squirted everywhere. Not able to hold back, I pushed my cock between her folds, rubbing her sweet nectar all over me. Her body was trembling from her intense orgasm.

Gripping my dick, I began to push inside her tight pussy. I felt her tense up when I had barely gotten the tip in. Leaning down, I took one of her fat, pink nipples in my mouth. I barely bit the tip and she moaned. Releasing it from my teeth, I leaned up and bit her bottom lip. She moaned again and pushed her pussy against my dick, gaining me another half inch.

I groaned and thrust my tongue in her mouth. She moaned and sucked on my tongue. Pulling back, I whispered in her mouth. “You taste that sweet pussy, baby?”

I pushed myself up and pulled my dick out a little bit. “This is going to hurt, but it’ll feel good in a minute. You’ll be squirting all over my dick in minutes.” Her eyes got huge, her hands gripped my forearms, and her teeth bit into her bottom lip before she nodded her head. With her consent, I thrust into her hard, tearing through her virginity. Her pussy clamped down on my dick so hard, I couldn't stop myself from coming all inside her. My balls got so tight, my spine tingled, and I came harder than I ever had.

I looked down and saw it leaking out of her along with the blood from her hymen. It blended together and ran down her sweet ass. I saw her little puckered hole tighten as she felt me looking at it.

I looked at her face and saw the tears leaking from her eyes. Fuck! It made me harden again. Leaning down, my tongue traced her tear streaked face. The salty tears had me ready to come again but I held back. I pulled out and thrust in again. I kept it going in slow motion until I sensed she was starting to enjoy, then I picked up my pace, circling my hips to stretch her out a little more.

God, she was so fucking tight. Her hands rubbed their way up her stomach. Something caught my eye while watching her rub herself. She had a fucking tattoo on her side just above her hip bone. The fact that she had a tattoo wasn't what got my blood boiling. It was the fucking fact that it was a tiny little devil and pitchfork with the script Devil's underneath it. What the fuck.

Closing my eyes and counting to ten, I reopened and continued watching the show she was giving me. Her hands continued their journey up stomach, finally reaching those large mounds. She began fondling her breasts, pinching her fat nipples. Growling I reached down and sucked them both into my mouth as she held them up, offering them to me.

The beast inside my head began clawing against my skull, begging me to choke her or hit her. It wanted more of her pain. I pushed it back, though. I'd already hurt her enough for today. I felt her clamping down on my dick and pulled out when she threw her head back, screaming in ecstasy. I wanted to watch that fucking perfect pussy squirt again.

Her sweet come shot out of her pussy like a fucking rocket. I bent down, lapping it up with my tongue. I licked her sweet cunt and eased my tongue down to her tight little ass. She tried to tighten her ass cheeks against my intrusion, but I used my hands to spread her wider. I kept licking a trail from her clit to her ass.

Soon, she was moaning and writhing again. Her fingers sought out her clit, rubbing it vigorously, searching for another orgasm. I reached my hand up and sunk three fingers in her sweet pussy, scissoring it. She bucked against me, still rubbing her clit. I kept my tongue on her ass, pushing against the tight hole.

Growling low in my throat, I pulled my fingers out of her and thrust my dick inside, bottoming out. My balls ached. No one had gotten me this worked up since that first whore I'd fucked and killed. I felt her pussy milking my dick. I grabbed her ass, lifting her up to fuck her deeper. I inched one hand closer to the crack of her ass.

She moaned, throwing her head back. Her hands were tangled in her hair, her eyes rolled back in her head. I eased a finger inside her tight little asshole. I was one knuckle deep, her ass tight and hot.

She tensed up and pulled away. "No, Mason." She pushed against my forearm, trying to make me leave that sweet ass alone. Deciding to appease her for the moment, I withdrew my finger. But, I'd definitely be revisiting that sweet spot. Gripping her hips, my hips pistoned as I pumped in and out of her tight little pussy.

She'd be sore tomorrow. I'd fucked her so hard this past hour that I doubted she'd be able to sit down the next few days without any pain. I couldn't stop the smirk that formed on my mouth at the thought. I'd be on her mind every time she did.

Her hands found my ass cheeks, clawing at them as she reached another orgasm. Her pussy squeezed, milking my cock spurring on my own climax. I pulled out of her and laid beside her. Her eyes were closed and her breathing evened out. I smiled. She had fallen asleep. I had wore her sweet ass out.

I traced her the features of her face with my index finger. My thumb rubbed her lips. I scanned her body, stopping when I saw the blood on her inner thighs. I rubbed it with my finger, sucking it into my mouth. I breathed deep after tasting the sweet, metallic taste of her virginity on my tongue.

The beast roared in my head, loving it.

Chapter Four

Reagan

I clenched my thighs together as Mason hit a bump in the road. I was so fucking sore. I didn't realize it would be this painful after. Then, again, I doubted most virgins got fucked as hard as I had. He'd been a fucking god in bed. I never imagined it being that good.

"I can take you home, Reagan. I don't want you fucking walking around in the dark." His voice had an underlying darkness lurking in it. I felt myself shiver in response. My pussy clenched, wanting him to dominate it again.

Shame also filled me. Mason lived in a damn mansion. I did not want him to see where I lived. He'd think the same of me as everyone else did. I liked the way his eyes stared at me with desire. I didn't want to see disgust or pity in his eyes.

"I'm not dropping you anywhere but home, Reagan. So, either you tell me where the fuck you live or I'll just take you back home with me." His eyes blazed at me, with what emotion, I couldn't decipher.

A sigh escaped me. "I live across the tracks in the trailer park. It's the blue trailer." I caught his nod out of the corner of my eye. I refused to look at him. I pulled my knees up against my chest, instantly regretting the motion when the pain came back. A moan left my lips and Mason's head whipped my way.

I saw the smirk on his face and wanted to slap him. He was enjoying this, the prick. I couldn't stop myself from rocking out and back the closer we got to my place. I glanced at the clock on his dash. My mom never gave me a curfew but the douchebags she kept around always tried to pull some form of fatherly bullshit. When we all knew it was just the power trip they enjoyed. A reason for them to be an asshole.

Mason turned onto the gravel road in the trailer park. Ours was almost at the end. He pulled into the small parking area in front. I sighed when I saw my mom's latest bastard's truck sitting there. Shit! This was going to be fun. Especially, after my hitting the fucker this morning.

The front door to the trailer swung open and he came out, squinting against Mason's headlights. Mason turned them off and killed the engine. The jackass crossed his arms against his chest and had a look of pure rage on his face when he spotted me.

"Is there a problem, Reagan? Is that your dad? Are you late or something?" Mason's voice sounded calm but his face showed hints of anger.

"I don't know. And hell no that's not my father. That's my mom's latest fuck buddy." I leaned towards Mason, my lips brushed against his lightly. He grabbed my face, pulling me closer. His tongue thrust inside my mouth, claiming me, dominating me, and making me want to climb onto him right here and now. I moaned, squeezing my thighs together. Even through the pain, I wanted him.

I pulled away before I made a fool of myself. "Bye, Mason." I opened the door and eased myself to the ground. I shut the door and didn't look back.

“Where the fuck you been, little girl? Out whoring around? Guess you get it honest, huh?” The smell of alcohol was hitting me in the face from the sorry bastard’s breath. I pushed past him and stepped over the threshold. That was as far as I got before he had his hands in my hair, slamming my head against the wall. Stars danced in front of my eyes, blinding pain shot through my face and head. I found myself falling to my knees.

I glanced around and saw my mom passed out on the couch. She was sporting a black eye and busted lip. There was dried blood below her nose. It made me question whether she was passed out from the liquor bottle on the coffee table or from this douchebag’s fists?

I had about ten seconds to take all this in before I got a harsh kick to my stomach. I doubled over, grabbing my stomach. My stomach churned and I found myself dry heaving. I couldn’t breathe for a second.

All of a sudden a loud roar filled the trailer. I heard a loud crash but I didn’t have the energy to look. The echo of flesh being pummeled sounded around me. When I had myself steady I turned my head toward the noise. Mason was on top of the bastard, punching his face. Blood was everywhere and Mason was like a machine. He never let up. The guy wasn't even fighting back. I didn't even think he was still conscience.

"Mason, you need to stop." My voice was so shaky. My whole body seemed to be quivering. I tried to stand but sharp pains shot through my abdomen at the sudden movement. My head wasn't too much better. Everything seemed to be swirling.

Mason had finally let up from pounding the guy's face in. Looking at him, I didn't think he even had a face left. Mason laid his hand on the guy's chest, like he was checking for a heartbeat. Whatever he felt, he didn't seem to like it. His face had a look of disgust upon it. He shook his head before a wicked gleam appeared in his eyes.

He grasped the guys neck and twisted. A sickening snap followed the motion. My stomach churned and I thought I was going to vomit. He had just fucking killed a guy. I'd lost my virginity to a murderer! Oh, God! Panic started setting in. Was he going to kill me, now? I was a witness. What about my mom? Surely, not. She's passed out. Mason looked my way and I froze. He smiled a panty dropping smile and winked at me.

He stood up, slung the guy over his shoulder and carried him out of the trailer. Taking a deep breath, I pushed myself into a sitting position, leaning my back against the wall. It hurt to breath. I bet that mother fucker cracked my ribs. I touched my face and felt blood coming from my nose.

Mason came back in and walked over to my mother. He put his fingers against her neck, checking her pulse. He looked back at me, nodding. Yeah, she was just passed out. He came my way, crouching down in front of me. His fingers trailed down my jawline. "He touched you, Reagan. No one gets to touch you." Pulling his shirt over his head, he used it to try to stop the blood flow coming from my nose.

He cupped the side of my face, his thumb gently stroking my cheek. "You're mine, Reagan. I protect what's mine. No one is ever going to lay their hands on you again."

He reached around my back with one arm and under my legs with the other, lifting me up. I laid my head against his shoulder, breathing in his scent. Closing my eyes, I let the blackness that kept threatening me take over. I didn't know how to process what just happen so I gave in and let myself drift off to sleep.

Mason

I pulled up at the house and glanced towards Reagan. Her poor face was bruised and bleeding. God, I could kill that fucker all over again. I clenched the steering wheel. The darkness inside me was clawing at my brain. My insides seem to be buzzing beneath my skin. It needed out. I looked over at her again. She looked so beautiful even through the bruising that marred her skin.

I got out of the truck and ran to her side. Gently as I could, I lifted her out and held her against me. I'd shot my dad a text so he was standing with the door open for me to enter without having to disturb Reagan. I carried her upstairs and laid her on my bed. I removed her shoes and jeans to make her more comfortable. I stopped to admire her beautiful cunt since she wasn't wearing any panties.

She was so fucking hot! I took a breath, my hands gripped my hair trying to shut him up. I couldn't fuck Reagan to distract myself. She was hurt. I needed to take care of her. I had to get a grip or I was going to do something I would regret. Crazy thoughts shot through my brain making my skull ache. I had to get out of here.

I threw a blanket over Reagan and left the room. My dad was waiting for me at the bottom of the steps.

"What's going on, Mason?" He sounded tired. A good son might feel guilty for all the shit I've pulled. Too bad I never claimed to be good.

"I killed the guy that was beating on her and her mom. He's in the bed of my truck. I'm going to toss him in the garage and then I've got to go out for a while. I need you to listen out for her til I get back."

I felt his hand on my shoulder. “Don’t do this, Mason. Think of her. If you love her, choose her.” I jerked my shoulder and his hand dropped. Without a backward glance I left the house. Tossing the body over my shoulder, I took him to the garage and smiled as I just threw him down. His body hit with a loud thump.

Turning back to my truck, I jump in and turn the ignition. Hitting the gas, I floor it out of the driveway and onto the road. Where to go? Where to go?

I decide to hit Mavis, the next town over. They have a shady strip club. No, I can’t do that. I need a nobody. I, also, can’t have witnesses. As I head down the highway, I notice a figure walking. Why would some chic be walking down the highway at this hour? Doesn’t she realize the dangers of walking the roads this late at night? I smile to myself and ease to the shoulder of the road.

Watching in my rearview, I can’t stop the grin that lights my face when I see her jogging towards my truck. She eases the passenger door open and meets my gaze. She has the biggest baby blues I've ever seen. Long, stringy blonde hair frames her face.

"Where are you headed?" I flash her my most charming smile. I watch her check me over and glance around the interior of my truck.

"As far as you'll take me." With that short reply, she hops in my truck and tucks bag in the floorboard between her feet. I try to ignore the whiff of body odor that hits me when she shuts the door. It leaves me wondering how long she's been walking? It's not enough of a stench to make me think she's completely homeless.

"So, what's your name?" I ease back onto the road. I watch her out of the corner of my eye. Her body is tense.

"Jess." Hmm... Wonder if that's really her name or just something she made up. Oh, well.

"I'm Mason. So, how'd you end up walking the roads at this hour?"

She just shrugs. Interesting. Most girls are all chatty. This one is intriguing me. Something about her makes me think of Reagan. I choose to shut that thought down. I will not let that change my mind. I've got to unleash the beast on someone so that I don't lose my shit in front of Reagan.

"Hungry?" I turn towards her and watch her swallow. She has a beautiful neck. She shakes her head but I know she is. Reagan pulled that same shit. I hit the steering wheel with my hand. Stop fucking thinking about Reagan. The girl jumps and leans towards the window.

"I'm sorry. I just remembered something I was supposed to do." I take the next exit and whip into a burger joint. I order two combos and ease up to pay. She's staring out the window, refusing to look my way since my fuck up.

I get the food and leave the parking lot. "Here, I got you some, too. I don't like to eat in front of people." She takes the bag and hands me mine. As I inhale my burger in a couple of bites, I see her in peripheral taking small bites, closing her eyes as if to savor the flavor. There's my good deed to her. I couldn't ease a sexual ache so I eased her hunger. Now, she was going to return the favor. She was going to help feed the darkness within me.

I know where an abandoned supermarket is, so I head that direction. She's still eating her fries when we pull in. I grab my, pretending to be texting. She finishes her food and puts the wrappers in the bag.

"Thank you, Mason." She sucks the straw in her mouth, washing down her food with coke. I let her finish.

"Hey, will you hop out of the truck and help me a second? I left something in the truck bed and I need help getting it." I almost laugh. Will she buy that line of shit? She just looks at me with those baby blues and nods her head. Apparently, picking her up and buying her food wins you her trust. That's just too bad for her.

I jump out and head around the truck. It's late and no one is really out. No one is definitely at this shithole. It's been closed for years. Graffiti has consumed the building and parking lot. When she's at the tailgate, I shove her against it. My hands close around her throat. Both her hands come up, pulling at mine. Her feet kick at my shins, but I push my whole body against hers, limiting her movement. When she continues to struggle, wriggling around, I shove us both towards the ground.

My body lands on hers, pinning her down. I lock both my legs around hers to keep them from lashing out at me anymore. I apply more pressure to her throat, watching her face turn red. Her eyes begin to water, her nails clawing at my skin. I keep putting more and more pressure. The veins in her forehead surface, her face begins turning a beautiful shade of purple.

That's it, sweetheart. Die for me. Her eyes begin to glaze over as the life slowly drains out of her. My cock hardens as her jaw goes slack and her hands fall to her sides. When I'm sure she's dead, I release my grip on her throat. I can't stop myself from grinding my hips into hers. There's so much pleasure in watching women die. I stroke the bruise forming on her throat from my hands.

Peace settles over me. The beast inside me goes back in hibernation. I stand up and pick up her body, tossing her in the back of my truck. Dear old dad will be so pleased.

Reagan

I woke up, my tongue feeling thick in my mouth, my head pounding, and I felt like my stomach was being stabbed by a thousand needles. Groaning, I opened my eyes and glanced around. It was so dark wherever I was at. The bed felt strange and yet, familiar. I tried reaching out to feel for my nightstand and found a warm body instead.

I froze, trying to think. I felt myself get nauseous again when the night's events came crashing over me. Fuck! What had I gotten myself into? I didn't know. Oddly enough, I wasn't scared of Mason. In a sick, twisted way, I was comforted by the fact that he had defended me and killed the bastard.

Sighing, I tried to push myself up and off the bed. I cried out as a sharp pain ripped into me. I felt Mason stir beside me. He was up and rushing around to my side of the bed, helping me up. "What do you need, Reagan?" His voice was rough from sleep.

"The bathroom." My voice sounded horrible. Mason nodded and swung me up into his arms, carrying me through the doorway of his bathroom. He gently put my feet on the floor and helped me with my pants. I felt embarrassment flood my cheeks. I had lost my virginity to Mason hours ago and he'd seen every part of me, yet, this somehow felt so humiliating.

He helped me down to the toilet and left the bathroom. I relieved my bladder and began the process of working my pants up when I heard Mason come back in the bathroom. "Reagan, I'm going to help you." His voice washed over me, comforting me. I couldn't stop the tears that ran down my face.

When he had my clothes back situated, he helped me wash my hands before sitting me on the counter. He gently began to wash the blood from my face and neck. A glass of water and a pill was placed in my hands. I sent a questioning look at Mason but he just urged my hand to my mouth.

Trusting him, I swallowed the pill and chased it with the water. Nodding at me, he lifted me back into his arms and took us back to bed. He laid me down and snuggled up to me. He pushed my hair behind my ear and placed a kiss on my neck. Resting his left arm across me, his breathing seemed to even out.

I lay there a few minutes, soothed by the sound of him sleeping. That pill started taking effect and I became drowsy. Before I drifted off, though, I heard the bedroom door open. Mason tensed next to me. I closed my eyes, so that I would appear asleep.

"The bodies have been destroyed. I hope she was worth it." It was his father's voice. What had happened to the body? Wait! He'd said bodies. Surely, that was a mistake, right? Why had he told his father? How do they act like this is no big deal? Those were my last thoughts before sleep overcame me.

I woke up feeling like shit for the second time within a six hour period. This time there was no warm body beside me. Mason's side of the bed was empty. The room was bright from the sun shining through the windows. I bit my lip against the agony in my stomach as I got up from the bed.

I went into the bathroom and blanched when I got a look at my face. My nose was swollen, a shiner had begun to form around my eye, my cheek was purple, my lip was busted, and there was massive bruising along my jawline. I pulled my shirt up and saw bruising there as well. Fuck!

I grabbed Mason's brush and tried to tame the tangles that were my hair. I searched through his drawers until I found an unopened toothbrush. After brushing my teeth and hair, I felt somewhat human. Thanking God for the hairband on my wrist, I pulled my hair up into a messy bun.

Leaving the bathroom, I walked to Mason's door and eased it open. I listened for a few minutes but heard no one upstairs. Walking to the edge of the stairs, I began the painful process of going down them.

I heard voices when I had made it down the stairs and towards what I assumed was the kitchen.

"What the fuck were you thinking? She witnessed you commit murder! Do you think she's going to keep your secret?

What if you piss her off? Quit thinking with your fucking dick, Mason!" His father's voice was borderline hysterical.

"Shut the fuck up, old man. Mind your own fucking business." Mason's voice was low. I couldn't see either one of them and didn't know if Mason was angry. I didn't want them to know I was there because then they would stop talking.

"It is my fucking business when I have to wake up Frank to dispose of the body! It's my business when word might get out that my son is a murdering psychopath! How the fuck are you so fucking calm? You've got the local MC's whore upstairs and murdered some bum that was fucking her mom and probably her! You've got to get rid of her! Tell me where I fucked up, son. Tell me where the hell I went wrong with you?" His father's voice broke up at the end.

"I'm not going to tell you again, old man! Shut the fuck up! And, keep my girl out of your mouth and out of your fucked up mind! Do you hear me, mother fucker? You'll stay the fuck away from my girl!" Mason's voice was full of menace. I heard a loud bang and some gurgling noise. I decided to make an appearance before I was found out.

I wasn't prepared for the scene before me. Mason had his father against the breakfast bar, his hand wrapped around his throat. He glanced up at me when I stood in the doorway. His nostrils flared and his eyes were dilated. Veins popped out on his forehead and neck. He had on jeans and a black wife beater tank. God, he was so fucking hot. His muscles were flexed and made my mouth water.

The violence in him both terrified and enthralled me. "Now, this is what's going to happen, old man. You're going to fucking call coach and tell him to excuse me for the day I missed at school and let me practice anyway. Is that understood? Because, I think we both fucking know what happens when I don't get to play. Don't we?" His voice dripped with venom.

I felt myself begin to shake. I didn't know what to do. I didn't dare move from my spot because I didn't know how Mason would react.

I watched in shock as his mother entered the kitchen, walked to the cabinet, withdrew a wine glass, and walked to the fridge. She filled it with three quarters of champagne and a dash of orange juice. She never even batted an eye at her son and husband. She walked right passed me without a single glance. What the fuck?

Mason let up Charles and walked towards me. I tried to relax when I felt myself tense up and hold my breath. His eyes lost some of the violence that seemed to always be lurking within them. A gentle smile lifted his lips when he stood before her. His fingers trailed down her jawline. I felt myself tilting my head towards his hand, basking in the affection he was giving me.

"How do you feel, Reagan? Are you in a lot of pain?" I felt my eyes tear up from the concern in his voice. How could he go from so much darkness to such sweetness in the bat of an eye?

I shook my head at him and felt my lip tremble. I was falling so hard for him and it terrified me. I hadn't known him forty-eight hours and I was in too deep. I probably needed to check on my mom. But, I didn't know if bringing her up was a good idea. Taking a deep breath, I decided to rip that band-aid off.

"Mason, I was wondering if it would be alright to check on my mom?" My voice sounded weak to my ears. I heard the slight tremble in my voice.

Mason cupped my face in both his hands, his thumbs rubbing my cheeks gently. "You don't have to ask permission, Reagan. Just tell me what you want and we'll do it, baby." He reached down and kissed my forehead. "Do you think you can walk to the truck or do I need to carry you?"

"I can walk." He gently pulled me against his chest, inhaling my hair. His lips kissed the crown of my head as his hands rubbed down my back.

He kept me against his side as we made our way to the front door. He walked slowly beside me, his arm never leaving my waist. After he opened the front door and closed it behind us, he swept me up in his arms and carried me to his truck. He only set me down long enough to open the truck door before picking me back up to situate me in the seat.

He was silent all the way to my place. When we pulled up outside the trailer, I felt myself get tense again. What was I going to say to my mom? And, what had she thought happened to her boyfriend or me for that matter? Was she even worried about me?

Mason came around to my side and helped me out of the truck. He carried me to my small porch. I opened the door and stepped inside.

"Where the fuck have you been, Reagan?" My mom's voice sounded from the kitchen. She was smoking her cigarette, her hand shaking. Her face was swollen and bruised.

Her eyes narrowed on me, her lips pursed. "What the fuck happened to you? Did Devil fuck you up?"

I felt Mason tense behind me and heard his swift intake of breath. "No, mom. You know I haven't seen him in a while. I'm dating someone new." I stepped forward, reaching back to hold Mason's hand as he came inside. "This is Mason."

Mom stared him up and down, not seeming impressed. Then again, she rarely was with anyone unless she thought she could get something out of them. She must have sensed that Mason wasn't going to take any shit from her.

"Did you do that to my girl?" Her voice tried to sound tough, but it lost some of it's edge. Did she sense the violence in him? Did she know she should be scared?

"No, mom. Mason didn't lay a finger one me. This was your lover boy's handiwork! I came home last night and this is what he fucking did to me."

Now, you would think a mother would be offended and ready to defend her child against someone that would harm them. Not my mom. Nope, not Cindy Smith. SHe just shook her head and rolled her eyes. "He was probably just punishing you for interfering in our business yesterday morning. Trying to teach you to mind your own business."

Taking a deep breath, I closed my eyes and pushed back the tears as my throat threatened to close up on me.

I turned my back to her and face Mason. "I'm going to grab some clothes if I'm going to be staying at your place. Unless, you don't want me to."

Mason's eyes bored into mine. "You're with me." His voice had no room for argument. I closed my eyes in relief. I did not want to stay here with her. I turned to make my way down the small hallway. I felt Mason behind me every step of the way. When we made it to my room, he glanced around. He laid his eyes on a bag in the corner and grabbed it, unzipping it. He went to my closet and just pushed all the clothes together and lifted the hangers up.

He threw them all in a pile on the bed. He emptied my drawers into the bag and zipped it up. “Anything else?” I shook my head. He threw the bag over his shoulder and grabbed the pile of clothes on their hangers. He left the room and I just stayed sitting on the bed.

When he came back in he stared at me, seeming to try to read what was going through my head. “You sure you don’t want to take anything else?” I shook my head. There was nothing else here that I wanted.

He nodded and kneeled down in front of me, his hands stroking my face. My eyes met his and I felt myself falling even more for him. His gaze was so tender and open.

“Let's get the hell out of here.” His voice washed over me and I felt safe. I felt at home with him. I nodded and stood up. He swept me up in his arms, carrying me out of mom’s trailer. I didn't even give her a second glance. Mason didn't even pause to shut the door. He stopped beside his truck, opening the door and setting me inside.

When he didn't move away from me, I looked at him. "You're mine, Reagan. Mine." He squeezed my thigh before shutting my door. He jumped up in the truck and we took off. He seemed to be a little happier than earlier. Not that any of his anger was directed towards me but he just seemed like something had lifted off his shoulders.

Mason felt my stare and looked at me. He smirked at me before turning his attention back to the road. "Something on your mind, Reagan?"

I took a breath and decided to just jump right into it. "I just don't know what exactly has happened. So, am I expected to live with you now? What's everyone going to think? Are you sure you want all this? And, why were you so angry this morning and now you're fine? I know I'm throwing a lot of questions your way, but I just want to know how all this is going to work." My hands were shaking and my stomach was a bundle of nerves. I couldn't help it. This was all happening fast. I couldn't believe he'd just packed up what little belongings I'd had and we were heading to his house.

Not that my situation had been any better at my mom's. But, I wasn't one of those girls that jumps right into a relationship with a guy and decide to move right in with them. I always said those girls were stupid. Now, I was one.

"Reagan, you're mine. So, I figure we'll skip right to it and you'll stay with me. My dad was talking out of his ass, so I set him straight. And, you're the reason I'm fine. You're the light for me. I've got a lot of darkness and you're my light." His voice sounded rough there at the end. I felt a tear leave my eye. That had to be the sweetest thing anyone had ever said to me.

We pulled up to his house and he asked me to sit here for a minute while he carried my stuff in. I watched him from my window. I saw his mom standing in the living room window. No expression was on her face. I didn't even know if she was looking at me or staring off into space. Sighing, I glanced towards the upstairs windows.

I spotted Charles staring down, shaking his head. He was not a fan of me. I just hoped it didn't prove to be an even bigger problem. Although, from what I had witnessed, Mason controlled his dad. I just couldn't figure what it was that his father was scared of. I knew Mason was violent but Charles didn't strike me as the type to be bullied. Something just didn't make sense.

Chapter Five

Three Days Later….

Mason was up and getting ready for school. Somehow, they had gotten a doctor's note to excuse me from school for this week and next. Part of his family's connections scared me and the other part gave me a sense of security. Mason came out of the bathroom dressed neatly with a pair of jeans and a polo shirt. His hair was styled and still damp. His scent was so delicious it made me want to moan.

We hadn't had sex since the incident that involved my mom's, now deceased, boyfriend. I know Mason wanted to. I felt his reaction to me every night when he snuggled up behind me, spooning me and every morning when he hugged me to him before getting out of bed.

I was still lying in bed, now, watching as he made sure he had everything. He walked towards me with a smirk on his face when he saw me squeezing my thighs together. His thumb rubbed my bottom lip before he lowered his head and pulled it between his teeth. His tongue licked where his teeth had been, soothing the sting. I moaned and tilted my head back.

Mason's eyes were watching my every reaction. "God, I want to fuck you, Reagan." His voice seemed to talk straight to my pussy, my clit throbbed.

"Why don't you?" Oh, how I wished he would. I ached for him.

"Because, I would hurt you. You need to heal before I fuck you again." His response making me ache for him even more. He gave me a quick peck on the lips.

"Now, I'm going to go talk to mom and make sure she can help you with some makeup to cover those bruises. That way when you're at the football game tonight, you want have everyone staring at you and running their fucking mouths." His voice had an edge to it and I knew he was worried about the gossip mill tearing into me. I wanted to tell him that they probably would anyway.

I was used to it. I had thick skin. I hated when he went to school without me, though. His parents both ignored me if they passed by me in the house. I tried to stay in Mason's room during the day. But, sometimes, I got antsy and needed to escape. I hated being cooped up all day.

He kissed me goodbye and made me promise to miss him while he was gone. Of course I was going to miss him. He was the only one I had to talk to these days. I closed my eyes and decided to nap to pass the time.

My nerves were getting the better of me. I didn't know why. I was riding in the passenger seat of Charlie's Lexus. Mason's mom was hidden away somewhere in the house and had refused to accompany us. She hadn't helped me with my makeup, either. I'd wandered around until I discovered her bedroom. I'd played around at her little vanity until I had covered all the bruises and marks that could be seen outside of my clothing.

I had even drew a little number ten on my cheek to represent him. I'd used some very expensive eyeliner to do it. Hopefully, Mason would love it.

I was wearing the football team's colors, red and black. I had on tight black skinny jeans, a tight red tank top, and black sandals. My tank top showed about two inches of my stomach and I had opted for no bra. I loved watching Mason's eyes when my nipples decided to harden for him.

I squeezed my thighs together and tried to think of something else. It was a little awkward getting all hot and bothered for your boyfriend while riding in a car with his father. I let out a sigh of relief when we pulled into the stadium's parking lot.

"I want to talk to you for a second, Reagan." I closed my eyes and restrained myself from groaning.

"I know my son is serious about you. That scares me. It should scare you. However, I realize that you don't know Mason that well, yet, so I'm going to try to help you with your decision. I want you to stay with us until you get all healed up. Then, I'm going to advise you to get the fuck out of my house and break up with my son. It's in your best interests, sweetheart. It would probably be in your best interest to hide out at your little MC's clubhouse afterward as well."

I couldn't stop myself from grinning at the asshole. I didn't even respond to him other than that. I opened the door and got out of his precious car.

Unfortunately, I couldn't leave the douche behind because I needed him to pay my way in. As if that little conversation hadn't been awkward enough, everyone stared as we descended the stadium steps to find a great viewing point. All the cheerleader bitches looked at me with a mix of loathing, disgust, and jealousy. That's right bitches, Mason is all mine.

I caught a look of lust shared between Charlie and one of the cheerleaders. It hit me that these two had fucked each other at some point. Nasty little bitch. Deciding to fight fire with fire and turn the tables on the bastard, I turned to Charlie. "So, you like to fuck cheerleaders, Charlie. Seems you like to dabble with the underage girls, huh?"

Anger lit his face before he schooled his features. His lips still showed his disgust towards me. "I've fucked a few of them, yes. Mason and I shared quite a few females before you came along." He smirked when he saw what that little bit of information did to me.

Shock, anger, and disgust filled me. So, Mason had fucked all the cheerleaders. Hell, apparently, he'd fucked a lot of women. Taking a deep breath, I told myself to calm down. That had all happened before me. And, obviously, I wasn't being offered to his dad. Not that I would allow that, anyway. But, the fact that he was keeping me to himself, told me that I was special to him.

Hell, I was sleeping in his house and we'd only had sex the one time. I nodded to myself. I was special to him. My heart rate finally calmed down and I felt confident in us.

I stood up when everyone started cheering as the football players made their way out onto the field. I caught Mason looking up in the stadium. I waved when he spotted me. He nodded his head towards me and I couldn't stop myself from smiling.

I thanked God when another older gentleman sat beside Charlie and kept him busy with conversation.

I was yelling and cheering by the end of the game. My man had scored so many touchdowns and got so many tackles that I caught myself laughing with pure joy. Charlie had even smiled at me a few times. I had really enjoyed watching Mason play ball.

I walked down to the bottom to wait on him to run by. All the football players were running by to hit the locker room. Mason spotted me and grabbed my belt loops, pulling me towards him. He jerked off his helmet and shook his sweaty head at me. I laughed as I pretended to try to get away from him.

His answering grin melted my heart. God, he was so sexy. "I love you, Mason." the whisper left my lips before I could stop it. His eyes dilated and he stared at me like he was ready to eat me alive. He growled before claiming my mouth. His tongue charged inside and dominated mine. His fingers dug into my hip.

He pulled away, rubbing his nose down my face. “I told you that you were mine. You’ll always be mine, Reagan.” He growled and kissed my cheek where I had written his number. His eyes scanned me up and down, lighting up when they landed on my breasts. My nipples were begging for his touch.

“God, I want to fuck you right here.” My pussy clenched at this words. His voice promising ecstasy. I press myself against him. His erection digging into me. I couldn’t stop the moan that passed my lips.

“I want to be fucked, Mason.” I lick my lips and get a shiver of pleasure as he watches the motion like a predator stalking his prey. There’s always something else lurking in his eyes. It’s always there just passed the sweetness, the desire, the anger. It’s almost like another soul inside him. Whatever it is seems dark, sinister.

"Be careful what you wish for, Reagan." Mason's hand clamps down on my wrist, pulling me behind him towards the locker room. Only we veered off to the right at the last second. We were on the other side of the building. Trees were all behind us.

Mason pushes me against the cement wall. I watch as he unhooks his shoulder pads and pushes them and his jersey off. His undershirt is the next to go. He unties his football pants, his heavy cock springing free. God, he is so fucking hung. I lick my lips with anticipation. I can practically taste him on my tongue.

Mason's mouth took possession of mine, his tongue sweeping inside. His hands lifted my shirt, my breasts spilling out. He growled and pulled away, his mouth closing over my nipple. I moaned and began undoing my jeans. Toeing off my shoes and wiggling out of my pants, Mason turned me around facing the wall. I placed my hands against the cement.

He got down on his knees and began placing kisses on my inner thigh. I heard him groan as he parted my folds, placing kisses on the cheeks of my ass before his tongue licked the lips of my pussy. It was pure ecstasy. I closed my eyes and thought I saw blinding lights dancing in front of me as his tongue swirled around my clit.

He sinks two fingers inside me and began working me over. I want him in me now. This is the sweetest torture. As his tongue continues its assault on my clit, his fingers fuck me. I can't hold back anymore. I push my ass out and grind on his face and hand. His answering growl urges me on. I pinch my nipples, the side of my face is pressed against the cool concrete.

I bite my lip to help keep us away from prying eyes. Although, right now, I didn't give a shit. I feel his thumb brush against my tight puckered hole. I squeeze my cheeks together against his intrusion. "I said no, Mason." It comes out breathy but I know he heard me. His fingers curl inside of me, stroking my g-spot. Everything goes black as I come so fucking hard.

I feel it drip out of me, running down my leg. I squeeze my eyes shut and feel my face flushed in embarrassment. Mason has no such qualms. His tongue seeks out the entrance to my pussy, lapping it up. His hands stroke up my body as he stands behind me. His huge cock pushes against my pussy. I moan when I feel the tip pushing inside me. I push back against him, taking him further inside me.

He growls, gripping my hips and thrusting all the way inside me. Pain and pleasure battle it out. I sigh and make myself relax. I don't think I'll ever get used to the size of his dick. Thoughts flee my brain as he begins to work himself in and out of me, his hips pistoning like a well oiled machine.

It's not long till I feel another orgasm building inside of me. My hand reaches back, gripping his tight buttocks. I can't stop the scream that leaves my mouth as I come again, hard. My whole body is shaking. I hear Mason's answering groan and feel his hot spurts of semen coating the inside of my pussy.

"Are you two about finished?" My head whips to the side at the sound of another voice. Charles, Mason's father is propped against a tree just staring at us. I try to cover my body with my hands. Mason pulls me against his body and turns us away from his father. His cock is still buried inside of me.

“Fuck off, old man.” His voice is still laced with seduction. I tilt my head up to watch his face. His hands are cupping my breasts, hiding them from the view of anyone else’s prying eyes.

“Mason, you need to wrap this shit up. Your team is going to be wondering where the fuck you are! Not to mention your coach will be crawling up both our fucking asses. We have fucking appearances to keep up, Mason! You can fuck her all you want at home!” I felt shame for a split second before the sinister look on Mason’s face sent chills down my spine.

His head slowly turned towards his father before cocking slightly to the side. I glanced towards Charles long enough to see his face turn ashen. His mouth opened and closed before he walked away from us.

I close my eyes wondering what I have gotten myself mixed up in. I take a deep breath before opening my eyes and staring into those probing green orbs. They seemed to stare straight inside my soul.

"Second guessing us, Reagan. Let me shut that shit down right now. You became mine the second you let me come in that sweet little mouth of yours, when you let me bust through that fucking pussy, and the second you stared me down with that whiskey gaze. And, the minute I can work it out, I'll be having that shit on your side covered up. Because, as I've said, you fucking belong to me!"

His mouth crashed on top of mine, his dick which was still buried deep inside me, twitched. Fear and need coursed through me, both battling for dominance. Mason pulled out and thrust back inside me, hard. It felt like he was pummeling my womb. Pleasure overrode the pain that it was causing. I whimpered when he flicked my clit with his thumb. My orgasm crashed through me when he pinched it.

His mouth descended on mine to swallow my screams. His hot cum bathed the inside of my pussy. His growls joined my moans as our tongues mated.

My legs were shaking when he finally pulled out of me. Emotions got the better of me as I stood there on display, his cum dripping out of me, and him scrambling to put himself back together. I felt so alone in that moment.

With my lip quivering, I began to fix my clothing and clean myself up the best I could manage. Mason turned back to me. His hands cupping my face. His teeth raked my cheek before nibbling on my bottom lip.

Pulling away, he grips my hand to tug me along behind him. Everyone has left at this point and I thank whatever deity is responsible.

Chapter Six

The parking lot is empty except for Mason's truck and a little sports car. Courtney, the cheerleader, is leaning against the side of it. Her eyes rake over Mason, before narrowing at our joined hands.

Mason doesn't even acknowledge her as he leads me to the passenger side of his truck. He lifts me inside, squeezing my thigh before closing my door. He's around to his side in less than a second. His door is opening when I hear her words. "Mason, we never fuck anymore! I want to know why! I know I'm a way better lay than that slut."

Mason lets out a dark chuckle. "She's the slut? Ha! Courtney, you had swallowed my cum and not even a minute later, you were slobbering all over my dad's dick! That makes you the fucking slut."

Shaking his head, he jumps in the truck and starts the engine. I sit quietly, digesting what I'd just learned. I lean my head against the window, the cool glass feels so good against my flushed skin.

The house is quiet as we make our way up to Mason's room. I head straight to his bathroom and turn on the shower. Shedding my clothes and stepping straight under the scalding water. I need to wash it away… the shame, the fear, his touch. Will I ever wash it away? Closing my eyes, I scrub at my skin until it feels raw. I inhale a shaky breath when I feel him behind me. I didn't even hear him come in. His hands trace a path down my spine and circle paths to the front of my hips.

Tears stream down my face but they become one with the droplets from the shower overhead. He'll never be able to see them.

His fingers pinch and pull at my nipples as his teeth rake my shoulder. His dick is pushing against my ass cheeks. When his hand makes its way to pussy, I cringe. I know I'm dry other than what water has made its way there. He's going to be mad. I can't help it. I fear this man that I worshipped before. A small part of me has always known that evil had made a home inside of him. But, there was another small part of me that hoped it would somehow die and disappear. The real terrifying thought was what had he done to cause such submission from Charles, such terror on his father's face.

Fuck, I'd witnessed him kill a man and not bat an eye. And, his father had helped him get rid of the body.

"Why aren't you soaked for me?Hmmm..." He strokes my pussy as his lips find my ear. "I'm going to fuck you, Reagan. I'm going to fuck you back into submission. I'm going to fuck you back into wanting me, loving me, and adoring me... "

He drops to his knees, rubbing the globes of my ass. I can't help the sigh that escapes as he kisses, licks, and nips my ass cheeks. I push my ass out to him, his groan making my clit throb. Why do I want this monster of a man so much?

I lay awake while Mason's even breathing tells me he's asleep. I gently ease out of the bed and head to his bathroom.

I quickly grab a change of clothes from inside the cabinet that I'd hidden there earlier. I jerk off the pajama bottoms and slide my legs in jeans. I throw the hoodie on over my tank top. Sliding my feet into converse, I tie them quickly, my fingers shaking.

When I'm finished I tiptoe out of the bathroom and make my way to his bedroom door. I open the door quietly and slowly pull it behind me without shutting it completely. Letting out a breath I'd been holding, I make my way down the stairs and jog to the front door. As I open the door, I feel someone looking at me. Mason's mother stands in the doorway of the living room. She winks at me and lifts her tumbler of booze to her lips.

Without a backward glance, I run out the door. I don't let up until I've reached my old neighborhood. I'm not far from the MC and I know Devil will hide me there until I feel safe.

Cutting through yards and down back streets I, finally, reach the compound that houses the MC known as Satan's Minions. I know that cameras are trained on me as soon as I step foot on their terf. I make my way to the back door and before I can lift a fist to pound on it, it swings open.

An older gentlemen wearing a cut without a shirt beneath it gives me a toothy grin. Chills go down my spine as I meet his cold stare. “Well, lookie here. You just going to stand there or are you going to state your business?”

Swallowing, I lift my chin and stare back at him. “I’m here to see Devil.”

A smirk tugs up the corner of his mouth. “These young studs always get the best pussy.” He turns his back to me and waves his hand for me to follow. We pass by rooms. Some have the door shut while others are open. Club members fucking women without a care as to who is watching them.

We made it to the bar and lounge area of the club. I saw Devil sitting on a stool with his back to us. Other members cast curious stares our way. Some of them recognized me, a few didn’t. The guy behind the bar said something to Devil and nudged his head in our direction. Devil turned towards me. His bright blue eyes nearly sent me to my knees.

A wave of relief hit me for some reason when he stood up, making his way towards me. His hand came up and cupped my cheek. “Sugar, what are you doing here?”

“I hate to ask this. But, do you think I could hide out here for a few days?” My voice shook a little. I closed my eyes and took a breath. When I felt steady, I looked back at Devil. His blue eyes were full of concern and a hint of anger.

“Why the fuck do you need to hideout?” His voice was calm yet held a lethal note.

“I just got in over my head with something and I need to lay low.” His eyes raked up and down my body a few times before coming back to my face.

He closed his eyes and pulled me to him. “You know you can always stay with me. You’re my girl, Reagan. The girl I can never have. But, my girl all the same.”

He stepped back and cupped his hands over his mouth. “Ok boys! My girl is going to be staying with us a little while. Hands off and treat her with respect.” A few of the guys groaned but otherwise gave their agreement. Devil grabbed my hand and pulled me through the clubhouse to his room.

He pulled a tshirt from his drawer and held it out to me. "You can sleep in this. The bathroom is through there but you know that." He adjusted his cock in his pants. "God, you still drive me wild not wearing a bra. Those gorgeous tits just a bouncing." He licked his lips and stepped towards me. "Can I just have a taste, Reagan?"

I wondered if I would still respond to him after having been with Mason. I nodded my head. He pulled me to him and his mouth descended on mine. His tongue swept inside my mouth, tangling and dueling with mine. He groaned and thrust his hips against mine. I moaned and rubbed back against him. I grabbed his hand and put against my tit, encouraging him to play.

I wanted to feel the insanity that Mason wrought on my body and brain, the unbridled passion. I felt some lust but it wasn't the same. I wasn't swept away. It was nice, don't get me wrong. It just wasn't the same. I felt tears build in my eyes but pushed them back. I didn't want to be a cock tease. Devil was doing me a solid and I had encouraged this.

He squeezed my tits and moved his hands to the button of my jeans. I could do this. His hand pushed inside my jeans. He let out a low growl when he found me commando. His fingers sought out my clit. He pulled away when I wasn't wet.

His eyes searched mine. "Sweetheart, don't get me wrong. I'm dying to be buried balls deep in that sweet cunt. But, I'm not going to fuck a girl that doesn't want my dick."

He was pulling back when we both froze.

"REAGAN!" Mason's voice echoed from down the hall. His growl sent shivers down my spine. My pussy pulsed, growing moist from his deep voice. Devil let out a slight growl of disapproval and pulled his hand away from clit. I watched in fascination as he slipped his fingers in his mouth, licking the moisture and closing his eyes.

"God, you taste exquisite. Too bad it's for somebody else." I closed my eyes against his wounded look.

"REAGAN, GET THE FUCK OUT HERE!"

Dear God, somebody was going to die tonight. A small part of me wished it were me. I knew either way I was going to hurt one of the men I held dear to my heart. I hated myself for that.

Chapter Seven

Mason

I'd followed her to this fucking MC clubhouse. But, not without some backup and insurance. I would tear this mother fucking place apart. The fuckers were letting me prowl through the place. Some seemed to fear me while others just didn't want to fuck with me after threats to this place, their freedom, their pals, and their fucking bikes. Yeah, that's right mother fuckers! I was holding all the cards right now.

I'd jumped down through a mother fucking skylight. I had small cuts all over me. My fucking left leg was killing me, but i pushed all of that shit down. I wanted my girl.

I threw doors open until I got to the lucky one that opened before I could touch it. I knew I was staring at my competition. The mother fucker was built and I guess to a chic he'd be attractive. I rolled my shoulders back and tilted my head. He smirked at me but not before I saw a bit of wariness pass through his eyes.

That was all I needed to know I was in complete control of this situation. He didn't know what to expect out of me. I shut down the rational part of my brain and let the beast out to play. A growl of rage left me when I saw Reagan's tit hanging out of the side of her tank top. What the fuck! I cocked my head to the other side as I studied her. Swollen lips, flushed cheeks, and the button undone on her jeans.

"You fuck my girl?" I saw a shiver pass over her as I spoke, her eyes glazed over. I smirked knowing I'd just turned her on.

"No, I didn't fuck my girl. You interrupted us with all that hollering you were doing."

I grinned at the cocky son of a bitch. "What's your name?"

He narrowed his eyes at me. "Devil."

Mother fucker! I let my gaze go back to Reagan. It went down her body and stopped on her hip. THe hip I knew had this mother fucker's symbol tattooed on it. She shifted on her feet and licked her lips as she stared back at me. I felt my cock straining in my jeans. I pushed passed Devil and went to my girl. My hand went between her thighs as I backed her up against the wall. I used my forearm to lift her up to eye level.

"YOu're mine, sweetheart. That sweet, tight pussy is mine. All of you is mine, understand? I don't fucking share." My lips descended on hers, swallowing her moans.

I knew he'd kissed those lips, but I couldn't help but claim her mouth as mine again. She needed to know who the fuck she belonged to. I felt her tremble against me, my forearm was getting moist from that sweet pussy. I growled low in my throat when I felt her nails sink into my shoulders. She was rocking against my arm.

Why the fuck had she left? Why did I let her drive me crazy? I could have any pussy I wanted. But, I wanted her. My other hand went to the fly of my jeans, I yanked the button loose and undid the zipper. I felt my heavy cock fall out.

Pulling my mouth from her, I gripped the beast between my legs. "You ready to be fucked, Reagan?"

Her eyes dilated and her tongue licked her lips. I watched as her nipples seemed to harden even more. “Pinch those pretty nipples for me, baby.” She did as I asked, moaning. I jerked her jeans down letting them settle down her ankles. She pulled a leg out of them. Pushing myself inside her, she threw her head back against the wall and let out a long moan.

“Are you fucking kidding me? YOu’re going to just fuck her in my room, in front of me?”

I pulled out and shoved back into her. Her juices flowing all over my cock. “Baby, do you care if I fuck you in front of him?” She shuddered and groaned as I swiveled my hips. She shook her head as her pussy squeezed my cock. I groaned and began pounding in and out of her. My lips went to her neck, kissing and sucking her sweet skin. My hands gripped the globes of her ass.

I let one of my hands ease it’s way to the crack of that luscious ass. One of my fingers rubbed the tight, puckered hole there. Reagan continued to moan as my cock punished her pussy. When I felt her orgasm tear through her, I eased my finger into her ass. Her eyes shot open and met mine. I shook my head at her as I worked my finger in and out. She clenched down on my finger as her pussy squeezed my dick.

God, I was going to fuck that tight little ass real soon. A part of me hated that the mother fucker was standing there watching us fuck. But, the sadistic side of me enjoyed him watching me pumping in and out of her tight little pussy. He needed to know that I had what he couldn't. I'd been the first to fuck her and I'd be the last fucking dick she'd ever taste.

That thought sent me over the edge. My semen coated the walls of her pussy. I bit down into her shoulder as I heard her answering moan telling me that she was coming as well.

I held her against me until I felt her body stop trembling. I helped her steady herself, fixing her jeans for her. "Get dressed, we're leaving." I rubbed her bottom lip. She closed her eyes and took a breath. I held mine as I waited for her to fight me on this. Tears built up in her eyes.

"I'll leave with you, Mason. But, we're going to have a talk." Her voice was barely above a whisper. It shredded something inside of me to see those tears in her eyes. I knew a part of me scared her. The beast that lurked within me. If she only knew she was the only one that was able to calm it. It stayed mostly dormant around her. I needed her. I loved her. I ached for her.

I nodded my agreement and waited for her to put her tit back in her shirt and to button her jeans. I pulled my hoodie over my head and settled it over hers. She pushed her arms through. The alpha male in me growled approval at her wearing my clothes. It hung on her but it made my dick hard again. When she was dressed, I grabbed her hand in mine and pulled her along behind me.

"She came here for a reason. I feel like I'm staring at the reason. So, I don't know if I should allow her to leave with you. I hope you understand." His voice tried to sound threatening, but it fell short. I knew he feared me. I, also, knew he'd try to act like a badass for Reagan. He wanted her. Hell, he'd be an idiot not to try to fight for her. She was the kind of female that would cause countries to go to war just to have a taste of her.

“Get the fuck out of my way. This is the last chance you’re going to get before I don’t play nice anymore.” I saw him stiffen. He was reacting to the menace that laced my voice. I ached to fuck this punk up. But, I wasn’t dumb. Reagan would lose her shit if she saw me crush him. That would have to happen later when I was alone with the fucker.

He stepped aside to let us pass. He grabbed Reagan’s hand when she was in the doorway. “If you need me, all you have to do is ask.” I watched as his thumb stroked over the knuckles of her hand. I heard the growl that left my throat. Reagan jerked her hand away and put it to my back to nudge me along. I smirked at him. It was cute that she thought she could control me. I’d let her be until I had her home.

We went to the main room of this shit hole. She gasped when she saw my father and the sheriff sitting at a table waiting on us. I just pulled her along behind me as they rose to follow us out.

I kept her hand in mine as we walked home. Just having her close kept me sane. The need to punish her clawed at my brain. I took a deep breath to keep it under control. I couldn't punish her right now. She'd bolt and I'd have to hunt her down again. I needed to earn her trust. Maybe, being honest with her would help with that. Closing my eyes, I decided to make myself vulnerable to her. "Reagan, I need to tell you something. I'm going to be brutally honest with you. Before you panic and run off again, I need you to hear me out and give me a chance. Can you do that?"

I watched her little nostrils flare and her tongue dart out to wet her lips. Not able to help myself, my lips crashed against hers and my tongue swept inside to play with hers. God, this girl fucked me up.

Pulling back, I let my guard down and stared into those whiskey eyes. I lost my soul to this girl and now whether she was going to guard it or crush it was the only thing that mattered.

"Ok." Her whisper swept over me. She was going to hear me out.

"I'm aching inside to punish you for leaving me, Reagan." She tried to pull her hand from mine. I held her steady. "YOu said you'd hear me out." When she sighed, I went on. “Something lurks inside me and you tend to calm it. I ache for you. But, another part of me aches to punish you and fuck you after. I can’t help it. I want to protect you from the world but I wonder who is going to protect you from me. I don’t know what to do. Without you I think I’d go mad. When you slipped out, it gutted me. It gutted me that you were running from me. And, the fact you ran to another mother fucking guy, slaughtered my insides.”

I took a deep breath to try to calm myself.

Her small hand cupped my face. I found myself rubbing against it. I closed my eyes when I saw the tear slide down her cheek. I was done for when it came to this girl. She held all the power.

“Mason, look at me.” Both her hands held my face, pulling me to her. She placed light kisses to my lips. I opened my eyes and saw fear in those gorgeous whiskey eyes. “I want you so much it fucking scares me. My insides are like jello when I’m with you. At the same time, I’ve never felt more safe with anyone. But, you smother me. I haven’t had a chance to breathe since you came along. I feel like I’m losing me. I want us to be together but, we don't have to be glued at the hip. I think I need to go home. We'll still be together just not living together."

I felt gutted. How the fuck could I let her go back to that abusive, shithole? Why would she rather live with that bitch of a mother than stay with me?

"Reagan, if I promised to back off a little, would you just stay at my place? I'd feel better knowing you were safe and being taken care of." He'd kept his voice low and calm. Inside though, a storm was brewing.

She closed her eyes and took a deep breath. "I need this, Mason. If there is going to be an 'us'. I need you to allow this to happen."

If there's going to be an us? What the fuck? There was always going to be a fucking 'us'! I felt my chest rising up and down rapidly. My nostrils flared with the need to unleash fury. But, I held it in check. I pushed all that shit down.

"Fine. Can I walk you home? I'll bring your stuff in the morning when I pick you up for school." I didn't look at her. I stared off behind her.

“Okay.” Her voice sound small and sad. I didn’t dare look at her, though. I was barely holding myself back from losing my shit.

We made our way through the rough side of town. As we headed to her trailer, I noticed all the lights were on and music was blaring from inside. Reagan slowed her pace and seemed to be second guessing herself. I chose to stay quiet. If she was going to back down, I wanted it to be her decision with no persuasion from my side.

We stepped up on her porch and she opened the door. There was laughter and the sound of someone moaning. We stepped into an orgy going on in the living room and a meth buffet in the kitchen. Reagan stepped back into my chest for a minute before trying to make her way to the little hallway that led to her room.

I glanced around at all the people inside to see who would pose as a threat. There were some good sized guys in the kitchen and one on the couch that was currently being rode by Reagan’s mom. Her head was thrown back in ecstasy as she pumped up and down on the guys dick. Another guy walked up to her, stroking his dick while he played with her tits.

She pushed her ass out towards him in invitation. No one had even noticed us yet. A skinny blonde walked up to me, rubbing her hand up my chest. “Wanna fuck, handsome.” I gripped her wrist before she made it far, applying enough pressure to make it hurt. Her eyes lit up with pleasure. This chic liked it rough.

“Fuck off.” I followed after where Reagan had gone. Opening her door, I found her laying on her bed staring up at the ceiling.

“You going to be okay here tonight?” I knew I wouldn’t be going anywhere. I’d camp out right outside her window.

“Yeah. Thanks for walking me home.” Her voice had a tremble in it. Tears had run down her face. I walked to her and settled myself between her legs, holding my weight up on my elbows as my hands cupped that gorgeous face.

“Hey, look at me.” Those whiskey eyes met mine and I felt my heart skip a beat. God, I loved this girl. She had fucking turned my world upside down and ripped my heart out of my chest just hours before. But, I'd fucking kill anyone that hurt her and set the world on fire just to see her fucking smile.

"I love you, beautiful. I'm just a phone call away. Do you want me to lay with you til you go to sleep?" She closed her eyes and took a deep breath.

"Will you stay with me tonight? I know what I said earlier and I'm standing by it. But, just tonight will you stay with me?"

My thumbs stroked her cheeks, my right one rubbed over her bottom lip. "Yes." I lowered my head, brushing my lips against hers before easing my tongue inside to taste that sweet mouth. Her hands rubbed up my back and dug into my shoulders as I moved my hips, stroking my crotch against that sweet pussy. She moaned inside my mouth as I applied more pressure. Her legs rose up and wrapped around my hips, pulling me closer.

I pulled away, gripping my shirt and shrugging it off. I stood up and stripped out of my jeans. I smirked as I watched how fast she removed her clothes. I gripped my dick as I watched those big, beautiful tits bounce.

It was probably terrible that I was going to fuck her with all that shit going on just outside her room. She was emotional and on the verge of some kind of breakdown. She had just ran away from me and I chased her down. Yeah, it was a dick move but right now, with that sweet pussy calling for me. Yeah, I was about to fuck the hell out of her.

As I positioned myself between her legs, I held back. Where had pulling dick moves been getting me with her? She was my girl, I'd claimed that sweet virgin pussy, and made her mine. But, she had left me. She was wanting space.

I sighed and closed my eyes. I bent down and slowly licked those luscious lips. "Reagan, are you sure you want this?" I placed light kisses over her lips, cheeks, and forehead. I nuzzled against her ear before licking along her jawline to that sweet spot on her neck. I lightly nipped at her neck, watching as she squirmed and sighed.

"Yes, Mason. I want you." Her hand closed around my dick, squeezing as she led it to her wet pussy. She rubbed the head against her clit and moaned. I felt sweat break out on my forehead. This girl was going to kill me. When she had me back at her entrance, I slowly pushed against her. The head of my dick entered her. It amazed me how tight she was after having fucked her about thirty minutes ago. She always felt tight.

I groaned when I felt her pussy clamp down on me. Thrusting hard, I pushed my way in to the hilt. She moaned, throwing her head back. I couldn't stop myself from feasting on those rosy nipples. I sucked one in my mouth as I pinched the other with my hand. Her hands gripped my head and pulled my mouth to hers. That sweet tongue of hers plunged inside and took over before I could think. I swivel my hips and her sweet moan spurred me on to continue.

My hands eased beneath her ass to lift her higher so I could go even deeper. I got a slow rhythm going, enjoying the feel of her sweet pussy on my dick, and that sweet tongue mating with mine. Her hands clawed at my head, pulling my hair as she came all over my dick. It wasn't long until I felt my spine tingle as my balls tightened and I was filling her with my cum. When I finished, I eased her back down on the bed, holding myself up on my elbows. I gazed down at the gorgeous face and those bewitching whiskey eyes.

I was going to marry this girl one day. She just didn't know it yet.

She closed her eyes, so I rolled to the side and pulled her against me. I was laying closest to the door. That way if one of those fuckers tried to come in, I'd give their neck a nice little twist and get back to my girl. She made a sweet little noise as she laid her head on my arm and went to sleep. I rubbed her back, slowly. I'd let her have a little freedom. Or, should I say, let her think I was giving her space. In reality, I'd be watching her every step of the way. She just wouldn't know it. My sweet Reagan.

Chapter Eight

Reagan

Six Weeks Later…

Mason was waiting for me outside to take me to school. I rushed around my room trying to make sure I had my books, keys, and phone. God, why had I overslept? My mom was yelling at me to hurry up. She was terrified of Mason and hated when he was here.

I left my room and headed towards the door when she stopped me. “You need to start meeting that creepy fucker somewhere else. I don’t want him anywhere near me! Do you hear me, girl? I said, I don’t want that mother fucker here again!” She gripped my hair and slammed me against the wall.

I reared back and let loose my elbow towards her face. I heard the crack before her scream echoed around the room.

Without looking back, I left out the door. Mason was making his way towards the trailer but stopped when he saw me. "What happened? I heard screaming." He paused when the door opened behind me.

"You little bitch! You broke my fucking nose!" I turned and saw the blood drain from her face when she spotted Mason. He pulled me behind him as he stepped up to the porch.

"And why would she do a thing like that Ms. Smith?" His voice was laced with malice. A chill went down my spine.

"I was just trying to talk her." My mom's voice wavered at the end. I snorted. My face still hurt from her slamming it into the wall. I was shocked my nose wasn't bleeding but my cheek had taken most of the impact.

Mason made a clicking noise with his tongue. "Ms. Smith, you're really starting to piss me off. Now, this is what is going to happen. Reagan is going to stay here until she decides otherwise. You're going to be polite to her. If she doesn't want you to talk to her, look at her, or even fucking breathe in her direction then you fucking don't!" With that he gave mom a little push against her shoulder. I watched entranced as mom backed away and Mason kept getting in her space. “You don’t want me fucking pissed. Do we understand each other?”

Mom nodded her head at him. Mason stepped back and came towards me. He put an arm over my shoulders and walked me to the truck. He opened the door and lifted me inside. His hands cupped my face, inspecting it. “Did she fucking hit you, Reagan?”

I shook my head as his thumb stroked my cheek. “I ran into a wall.” I leaned forward and licked the seam of his lips, distracting him. He narrowed his eyes at me before sucking my tongue into his mouth, causing me to moan. I wrapped my legs around his waist pulling him into me.

I tore my mouth away before I lost myself completely in him. I had something to discuss with him.

“So, a good friend of mine reached out last night and asked me to meet her at some concert a few towns over. I’m going to meet her there tomorrow night.” I kept my voice strong. I knew he was going to object to my going alone. I was just waiting for it to sink in.

“Okay, what time do we need to be there and I’ll pick you up when you’re ready.” Oh, boy. He hadn’t caught on.

“Mason, I meant just me. You know, girl time.” Although, he may not be as understanding if he knew her and I had ate each other out while Devil had watched jerking himself off. That is until I’d helped him finish the job in my mouth while Avery had continued licking me.

“Hey, what were just thinking about? Your face got all flushed. What the fuck is really going on?” Mason had just went from zero to sixty. I had fucked up.

“I was just thinking back to a night her and I had gotten a little playful with each other.” I shrugged trying to play it off and hoping the thought of two girls together would distract him from any other thoughts he was having. I was going to win this fucking battle.

Mason’s eyes darkened with lust. I felt his erection pushing against my pussy. I ran my fingers through his hair. “If you’re a good boyfriend and let me go, by myself. Maybe, we can put on a little show for you after." His hands went to my tits. He squeezed my bra-less girls, his fingers pinching my nipples. I moan and rub against that hard dick.

"Baby, I don't like to share." His mouth crashed on mine and I was dry humping his erection like a fourteen year old girl during a make out session. He pulled away and stroked my face with his thumb. He stepped back while I tried to readjust myself in a daze. Shutting my door, he came around and jumped in the driver seat.

He drove us to school in silence. I went through the motions of a school day. I realized during my last class that he had never given me an answer.

I met him at his truck in the school parking lot. My heart started pounding when I saw him making his way to me. He was so tall, handsome, and just had that air about him. His muscles made his clothes cling to him, the way he had his backpack slung over his shoulder, with his forearm holding the strap just did something to me. I know that sounds stupid, but he just looked so fucking good. A part of me saw red when I noticed the other girls checking him out as well.

As he got closer, I reached out, wrapping my arms around his neck and pulled him in for a kiss. He growled low as my tongue plunged inside his mouth. It sent a live wire straight to my clit. I felt myself grow wet. I pressed my body fully against his. God, I wanted to fuck. He'd left me hanging this morning and I really needed some dick.

He pulled away and smacked my ass. "Get in the truck, babe." He threw his backpack in the back and hopped in the truck.

As soon as he slid inside, my hand went to his zipper. I released his heavy, massive cock. Leaning down, I licked the pre-cum off the tip. I moaned as the salty taste lit up my taste buds. Mason growled low in his throat as he started the truck. I took all I could of him in my mouth, hitting the back of my throat. My pussy flooded as I gagged. His hand gripped my hair and pushed my head down to take even more of him. I couldn't handle all of him, he was just too much. My hands gripped his thighs as my head bobbed up and down, working his cock. My tongue stroked just beneath the head, making him groan.

My other hand worked his base in sync with my mouth. It wasn't long till I felt his cum coating my mouth and throat. I moaned and swallowed every drop while continuing to work him. When he was finished, I sat up meeting his hooded gaze. I licked my lips and watched as his eyes followed my tongue.

Pulling my shirt up and over my head, I stroked my nipples. Pinching them lightly before bringing one of my breasts to my mouth and licking my nipple. "Wanna fuck me, Mason?" It wasn't long before he was pulling to the side of the rode and pulling me on his lap. His mouth latching on to my tit and sucking my nipple into his mouth. I unbuttoned my jeans and pulled away to take them off.

He groaned when he saw I wasn't wearing any panties. "God, you fucking kill me. No bra and no fucking panties." He grabbed me, slamming me down on his cock. No matter how many times he came, he was always hard for me again. I threw my head back moaning as he stroked my clit with his thumb. He gripped my hips, guiding me up and down on his cock. I grabbed his hair and sucked his bottom lip into my mouth.

Using the steering wheel to hold onto, I took over, riding him hard and fast. His hands gripped the cheeks of my ass. It wasn't long til we were both coming.

I stayed on him long enough to thoroughly savage his mouth with my tongue. When I pulled away, he was looking at me like he worshipped me. I couldn't stop myself from grinning. I had just fucked his brains out.

Putting my clothes back on, I looked over and noticed he hadn't moved. Just continued to watch my every move.

"What's wrong, Mason?"

"I fucking love you, Reagan." His voice was hoarse and his eyes were glazed over. I reached my hand out and stroked his cheek.

When I didn't answer him back, he closed his eyes and began putting his dick back in his pants. He jerked the truck in drive and drove me home. I knew what he wanted and I did love him. But, he was intense and obsessed with me at times. So, I was trying to tread through our relationship carefully. I didn't want to give him any more power over me than he already had.

His truck came to a stop in my driveway and he began tapping his finger on his steering wheel. “How did you plan to get to that concert?”

Shit. I hadn’t thought that part through yet. “I don’t know yet.” I didn’t look at him as I spoke. I figured I would bum a ride from someone.

Mason’s sigh sent a chill down my spine. “So, you wanted me to be alright with you going to some fucking concert that you have no fucking clue on how you’re getting there and back?” I still didn’t look at him. I just shrugged my shoulders. I reached for the handle of the door, deciding it would be better to just ask forgiveness after I went than keep this conversation going.

He gripped the wrist of my other hand, applying pressure when I still refused to look at him. “Reagan.” My name on his lips made my clit throb. I closed my eyes, taking a deep breath. When I met his gaze, I had to lick my lips. The fire in his gaze caused both fear and lust to flood my veins.

“Don’t look at me like that or the only place you’ll be going is down on my dick again.”

“Mason, I don’t know, okay? I’ll fucking figure it out.” I went to get out again when he pulled me back again.

“Why can’t I fucking take you and pick you up when it’s over?”

I couldn’t stop the sigh that left me. “Because we both know you won’t fucking leave.”

He let me go and rubbed at his forehead. “Would it be so fucking terrible for me to be there? I don’t get why you want to keep me away so fucking much?” He threw his head back against his back glass. “Just get the fuck out of my truck.”

My lip trembled. My hands shook as I grabbed my back and got out. I slammed the door, making myself look forward. I wasn’t going to give him the pleasure of me looking back at him. Mason never treated me like that. Had I finally pushed him completely away? I was at war with myself when it came to him. He made me fucking crazy.

I ran up on the porch and jerked the door open before the tears began to fall. I shut the door behind me and found myself walking to window to see if he was still there. He sat there in his truck staring at the trailer. I watched as he punched the steering wheel over and over. His hands gripped his hair before he slammed the truck in reverse.

His tires spun as he sped out of there. I sank to the floor crying. This was what wanted, right? Fuck! I felt a hand on my back and jerked.

I turned and saw my mom looking at me. Her eyes, although black from my hitting her this morning, held compassion. For once, I felt like she loved me. She hesitated for a few seconds before hugging me. Her hands rubbed up and down my back. “It’ll be okay, honey. You’ll see.” I let my tears flow freely and cried it out.

When the well dried up, I pulled back and looked at her again. “Thank you.” She smiled at me and helped me stand up.

“Why don’t you go shower and you’ll feel good as new.” She went to the couch and lit a cigarette. I didn’t know how to deal with this side of my mother. I walked by her and straight for the bathroom. Pulling my hair up on top of my head, I got in the shower. I washed the smell of Mason off my body and scrubbed my face.

Chapter Nine

Stepping out of the shower, I wrapped a towel around me and looked at myself in the mirror. My amber eyes were shining back from all the crying. They were a little puffy. A cold washcloth and a little makeup would hide all that, though.

"You're a strong, bitch, Reagan. No matter how hard you're knocked down, you always get back up! This time is no fucking different." I smiled back at myself. I walked to my room and began getting ready for the concert. I chose extremely destroyed skinny jeans, a white tank top that had a hole in the middle of the chest that would show a hint of my girls, and my red chucks.

I dressed quickly and applied my makeup. Letting my hair back down, I brushed it out and took the straightener to it. I put some big hoops in my ears and looked myself over in the mirror. My nipples showed through my white tank and I smirked. I loved making people crazy. Mason would growl at me if he saw it.

I left my room and my mom's eyes turned the size of saucers as she looked me over. "Does he know you're leaving the house like that?"

I let out a little laugh and shook my head. Feeling completely reckless, I shoot Devil a text asking if he could spare a prospect to give me a ride. I smile when he replies almost instantly with a 'yeah'. I tuck my phone in my back pocket and decide to wait on the porch. I didn't want to push my luck with the slight truce my mom and I had going on at the moment.

About twenty minutes later I hear the rumble of a motorcycle. My heart skips a beat when I see it's Devil instead of a prospect. Fuck! I might could've gotten by with a prospect. But, if Mason found out I had rode on the back of Devil's bike to the concert, he would fucking paint the town red with the MC's blood.

I walk over to Devil. "I asked for a prospect, Devil."

He smirks at me. "Darling, there's no fucking way I'm letting you press those tits against one of those little dick's backs."

I can't stop the laugh that leaves me. I climb on the back and wrap my hands around his back as we rumble down the road. The wind flows through my hair and over my face. I lay my head against his back and close my eyes, enjoying the freedom of being on the back of a Harley.

It takes us a little over an hour to arrive at the concert. People are all over the place. It's an outdoor concert being held in pretty much a wide open field. There's about ten different bands playing tonight. It's going to be fucking awesome.

"Thanks for the ride, Devil." He grabs my arm as I start to walk off. His thumb rubs my hand.

"How you getting home, Darlin'?"

"I'm sure I'll catch a ride with Avery." I bite my bottom lip as I see his eyes glaze over with lust. I know he's remembering our little semi-threesome. He pulls my hand to his crotch rubbing it over his hard-on.

"See what you do to me, Sweetheart." I laugh at that.

"I don't think that's all me. I think Avery is part of that erection."

His eyes grow series. “No, Sugar. That’s all you. Watching her lick that sweet pussy of yours. The flush of your face as you came. Then, when those fucking lush lips wrapped around my dick sucking me till I came. Fuck. It was all you, Reagan.”

I felt myself getting heated and pulled away. I couldn’t get wrapped up in Devil right now. He was trouble. I knew he loved and wanted me. But, he’d never put me above the club. They always came first. I wasn’t going to be second anymore. Not after getting a taste of being the object of someone’s obsession. Mason had ruined me in that sense.

“I gotta go meet Avery. Thanks for the ride, Devil.” I lean forward and kiss his cheek before walking away.

Making my way through the throngs of people, I finally spot my slightly crazy friend. Avery is holding two beers and chatting up a group of guys. She’s wearing leather pants, combat boots and a lime green bra. Her tits are a little bigger than mine, so they’re almost spilling out of her bra. Her hair is black and styled in a short pixie cut. She has bright blue eyes, a pert little nose, and thick lips that make the guys drool.

I whistle at her. Her eyes going straight for me. She looks me up and down, licking her lips. I'm straight. I only dabbled with her to fuck with Devil, not that I didn't enjoy it. But, Avery swings both ways. And, she was really into me for a while. It kind of broke her heart when I wouldn't pursue an affair with her.

"Hey, babe." I stand beside her and she hands me one of the beers. The guys all give me leering looks. Sorry, boys. Definitely, not interested.

I nod and answer with short replies when they talk to me. Suddenly, the music starts and I pull Avery towards the stage.

We make it through about seven songs and twelve beers when she hands me two pills. "What are these?" I stare down at them in my hand.

"Just a little something to help you relax." SHe winks at me.

"I'm already relaxed." I was. I had a nice little buzz from the beer.

"Just take them. I promise they'll make you feel even better." What the hell. I'd had a shitty day. I pop the pills and chase them with the rest of my beer. "I'm going to get another beer." I walk through the crowd towards the beer guy. He fills a cup to the rim and hands it to me.

I drink from it a minute, standing away from everyone. Just swaying to the music. I close my eyes and let go. My body feels really flushed. I run my hand over my face and moan. God, that feels good.

I feel a hard body at my back. "Baby, what the fuck did you take from her?" I groan and lean back into Mason. His arms envelope me, his hands settling on my stomach. I rub my ass against him, wanting more. I push one of his hands towards my pussy, rubbing it against me. God, I was about to fucking climax.

He spins me around to face him. "Reagan, look at me. What did you take?"

His green eyes pierce mine. He was so fucking gorgeous. He smiles slightly and I realize I said that out loud. I moan as his hands grip my hips. “I need to fuck, Mason. I need to fuck so bad.” I feel my legs trembling.

“Fucking bitch. She gave you fucking ecstasy.” His grip tightened. He moved his hands up my sides, making me moan. “I don’t like you wearing that fucking top out here, Reagan. I see your fucking perfect, pink nipples. Not to mention you can see your actual tits through that mother fucking hole. There’s practically nothing to those jeans, either. God, you make me fucking crazy.” He was stroking the underside of my tits, making me crazy. My body needed to be touched all over and I needed to come so bad.

“There you are, girl! Who is your friend?” I hear Avery behind me. Mason growls low in his throat. I look up and see the menace lurking in his eyes. I try to turn towards her but he holds me firm.

“Why the fuck you feeding my girl ecstasy, bitch?”

“Excuse me.”

“You fucking heard me, cunt.”

“Reagan, are you going to let him talk to me like that? What the fuck?” Avery grabs at my arm and I throw my head back moaning. She purrs in my ear. “You feeling good, honey?” Her hand trails down my arm until it’s snatched away.

“Fuck off!” Mason’s voice sends a bolt of lightning straight through my body. I grind against him until I hit the right spot and orgasm right there. I can’t help the loud moan that escapes me. I feel tears hit my cheeks as I continue mewling from the pleasure.

“You can have us both if you want. It’s not our first time fucking in front of a guy. It’s kind of our thing.” I see red when Avery rubs up Mason’s arm. I don’t know what comes over me as I’m suddenly punching my friend over and over in the face. Her screeches finally penetrate my jealous fog. I pause for a second and her fist catches me off guard as she flips us.

She’s on top of me punching my face for a second before she suddenly disappears. I lay there stunned. What the fuck just happened?

I touch my face. I pull my hand back and stare at the blood on my fingers. Is that mine or hers? My hands go to my hair and my senses become overloaded. Too much is racing through my brain. I can’t hold onto a thought. Pleasure and need is at the forefront, though. God, I'm fucked up. Mason. Where did Mason go? A feeling of pure euphoria envelops me and I moan.

I'm lifted from the ground and thrown over a shoulder. The scent tells me it's Mason. His hand is stroking my ass as he carries me away. I glance towards the trash cans near the portable toilets. I see Avery propped up, her head at an odd angle. What was she doing? Mason grips my ass cheek and all thoughts leave me as I grind against him.

We reach his truck and lays me on his tail gate. He jerks my jeans off my body and buries his face in my pussy. His tongue swirls around my clit before he sucks on it. I scream as another orgasm tears through me. "Is that what you wanted, Reagan?" His hands reach up and tear my tank in half. My tits bounce and his lips settle around a nipple. He bites down and I feel myself tremble.

He pulls back staring at me with lust filled eyes. He shakes his head. "We can't do this shit here. Someone might see you and then I'm going to lose my shit." He picks me up and settles me inside the cab of the truck. Shutting my door he jogs around to the other side.

"Wait. Mason, what are you doing here?" My voice trembles. My body is like a live wire. Everything sets my skin on fire. The seats are sticking to my skin. I rock out and back trying to find relief. I moan and close my eyes against the sensations. "What's wrong with me?" I feel tears roll down my cheeks.

Mason grabs my face, turning me towards him. "Look at me, baby."

I open my eyes and meet his gaze.

"You were drugged, baby. That bitch dosed you with ecstasy. You're going to have to let it run its course. You shouldn't trust people so easily."

I rock out and back, rubbing my hands over my bare legs. My hands roam up my torso to my breasts. It feels so fucking good. Mason's growl stops me.

His hand grabs mine, intertwining our fingers, and squeezing gently. It seems to ground me a little. Maybe I would survive this pleasure filled hell.

Chapter Ten

Mason

She was making me fucking crazy! Watching her rub herself, moan, and look at me with those whiskey eyes were torturing me in the best fucking way. This was the ultimate fantasy for a guy. There was just a few things hovering over it like a fucking dark cloud. The fact that she rode on the back of that mother fucker's bike to the damn concert instead of letting me take. Also, that she fucking took drugs from that stupid cunt.

Bitch got what was coming to her, though. Hope it was worth it for her. I stroke her hand until we get to my house. She refuses to let me go, so she climbs over to get out on my side. I throw her over my shoulder and carry her through the house and up the stairs. I can't stop myself from slapping her ass a couple of times. She lets out a sexy whimper each time.

When we reach my room, I kick the door shut and throw her on my bed. Her tits bounce as she lands. I shrug out of my clothes in record time.

Her hands are between her legs, rubbing against her clit. I grip my dick, stroking and watching her play with that sweet little nub.

“Reagan, get on your knees.” She moans and raises up to her knees. I walk over to her and rub my dick against her tits. “Now, on all fours and open that pretty little mouth.” She takes me into her mouth. Her lips squeeze the head of my dick before working her way down. She can’t take all of me but what she can handle feels fucking awesome. When I hit the back of her throat, I groan.

I lean over and play rub the cheeks of her ass while she continues sucking me. I dip two fingers into that sweet pussy. She begins riding my fingers and moaning around my dick. I feel my balls tighten as I wiggle my fingers, hitting her g-spot. She whimpers and sucks harder. I stiffen and let my cum fill her mouth. She swallows it all like a pro.

She's still riding my fingers as her mouth releases my dick. When she comes again, I pull my fingers out of her and rub her juices all over her tight little ass. She moans and rubs against my fingers. I keep getting rubbing before pushing a finger inside that tight little hole. When she moans again, I slide my body behind her to play. I use my other hand to fuck her pussy while I keep playing with that ass.

I finger her ass for a few seconds before working in a second finger, stretching that little ring of muscle. She stiffens for a minute before throwing her head back when my other hand strokes against that g-spot. I smile knowing I'm going to get to fuck that ass tonight. Do I know she'll fucking hate me for it in the morning? Yep. Do I fucking care? Nope. She fucked up twice today.

I add a third finger and really start finger fucking her ass. I slip my other hand out of her pussy and rub her clit. She's enjoying every dirty little second of it. Her screams fill my room. My dick is throbbing. I push into her pussy, stretching her with my size. She pushes back against me before throwing her head back as she comes again. I pull her hair as I slam into her hard.

I scissor my fingers inside her ass, trying to stretch her as much as I can before I put my dick in her. God, she's going to be so fucking tight. I have to pull my dick out of her pussy before I blow my load just thinking about that ass. This girl has me all sorts of twisted.

"Reagan, I need you to relax for me baby. I'm about to fuck you so hard. It's going to feel so fucking good, okay?"

She moans and pushes against my fingers. I slide them out and position the head of my dick against her ass. I rub her juices all around it, my dick still wet from her pussy. Sweat beads all over my forehead as I go super slow pushing the head inside her. She's so fucking tight. When I feel her stiffen, I reach around rubbing her clit again. I know she won't be able to take all of me but I'm going to make her take all she can.

I keep pushing, stretching her tight ass. When I'm in as far as she seems to be able to take, I stop, letting her adjust. My fingers keep stroking her clit until I feel her begin to tremble with orgasm. Her ass tightens around my dick as she comes. I pinch her clit making her scream as I pull out and slam back in. I can tell by the noises she's making that she can't decide whether she likes it or not.

My hips swivel as I try to open her up more. "Your ass is so fucking tight, Reagan. I'm not going to last." I only last a few more strokes before pulling out of her. "Turn around fast, babe." She flips around and looks up at me. "Open up." She opens her mouth as I stroke myself. My cum lashes against her face, some of it landing in her mouth. She licks her lips and swallows. God, she's a fucking wet dream.

She'd make an awesome porn star. That thought scares me a little. I don't want her fucking any other guys. That's my pussy.

I go in the bathroom and wash my dick off. When I come back out, she's laying on her back playing with her pussy. Fuck. She's going to be so sore tomorrow. I decide to have another round with her and then I'll give her something to knock her ass out.

I use warm washcloth I got for her and wash her face off. Then, I kneel between her thighs and stare at the perfect pink pussy. I growl before tonguing that sweet clit. Her hands grip my hair pulling my face closer. It's not long before she's actually fucking my face with her pussy.

I stand up and slam my throbbing dick inside her. I fuck her til she comes all over my dick. In the back of my head, that ass is taunting me. I pull out of her, throw her legs over my shoulders, and push my dick back in that tight, hot ass. "I'm addicted now, babe. I'm going to have to fuck it all the time."

THose big titties bounce up and down, those whiskey eyes are dilated and staring up at me like I'm a fucking God. Her ass squeezes down on my dick and I watch in surprise and her pussy squirts. She loves me fucking her ass. That sends me over the edge and I fill that ass with my cum. I pull out and watch as my cum slides out and down the crack of her ass. "You're so fucking hot, baby. So fucking hot."

After I wash off again, I find some sleeping pills in the medicine cabinet. I take them to her with water. "Here, these will make you all better." She doesn't take them from me. She looks up at me and opens her mouth. God, she was going to be the death of me. I put them on her tongue and she swallows them without the water. I can't help myself. I grab her face, thrusting my tongue inside her mouth, claiming her.

We keep kissing til I feel her relaxing against me. I could fuck her all night but I know she's already going to be fucking sore tomorrow. I pull away from her and rub her back til her breathing evens out. She looks like a fucking angel laying there. I can't stop myself from rubbing her all over. My dick is hard within seconds as I trace circles around those fat nipples. I straddle her, put my dick between her tits, and push those gorgeous things together. I thrust in and out, my dick hits her chin a few times and that just turns me on more. A few more hits has those whiskey eyes gazing up at me.

"I'm sorry babe. These luscious girls were taunting me." I feel my balls tighten when she smiles up at me. Her pink tongue comes out of her mouth trying to lick the tip. I stop and let her suck the head in her mouth. I groan when she swirls her tongue around and around. I pull out wanting to cum all over her.

I feel it at the base of my spine, my balls tightening. I let out a groan when I felt each rope of cum jetting out. It lashes her breasts over and over. When I'm finished, I rub my dick all in it. I can't stop myself from slapping each tit which makes Reagan moan. When my dick is covered in my cum, I rub it all over her pink lips. Her tongue comes and licks me clean. On instinct, I thrust into her mouth until I hit her throat.

Sighing, I quit before I'm fucking her again. She really needs to sleep that shit off. "Go to sleep, babe." She shocks me as she lifts her tits to her mouth licking my cum off. Fuck!

"I don't wanna sleep. I wanna fuck." She bucks her hips off the bed to show me how much. God, she's such a dirty girl.

"If I fuck you anymore you're not going to be able to walk tomorrow." I get off the bed to go get something to wash those tits off.

When I come back out she's bent over with that tight little ass in the air. Fuck! Her hand is between her legs, fingering her pussy. I watch as she pulls out and rubs her glistening fingers over that puckered little hole I was fucking earlier. "You want to fuck my ass, Mason? Fuck me like I'm a dirty girl!"

I lean down and run my tongue from her clit to her ass. “You are a dirty girl.” I suck on her clit and listen to her moans. “This is the last time I fuck you tonight, Reagan. Okay?” She pushes back against me. I slap her ass hard and watch as she gets sopping wet. Fuck. I rub my dick up and down her slit. Her hand reaches back clawing at my hip.

“Fuck me!”

I thrust into her pussy. Her walls clamp down on my dick and I realize that she’s already coming. Damn. I was going to make her come before fucking her ass again. Mission accomplished. I pull out and start rubbing my dick against the tight little hole I want to fuck hard.

“I’m going to tear this ass up, baby. I have a feeling it might be the last time I get to fuck it for a while.” I push against it, easing in slow. God, it’s so tight and hot. She moans and pushes back against me, helping me slide in even further. She’s such a dirty bitch. I fucking love it.

Gripping her hips, I thrust in and out of her tight ass. It grips me so tight, I know I’m not going to last. I just can’t get enough of her. Somehow, no matter how many times I fuck her she always gets me right back hard and ready to explode. She keeps pushing back into me when I'm pulling out. A few more thrusts and I'm filling her ass full of my cum. Fuck!

Sweat is dripping down my back and forehead. I need a shower. I slap her ass and head to the bathroom. When the water is steaming, I step under the spray. I'd do anything for that girl out there. I'd already killed for her twice. She was going to be my wife one day soon. She just didn't know it, yet.

I dry off and head back to bed. I smile when I hear her lightly snoring. It's adorable. I pull her against me and close my eyes. Tomorrow was a new day and we were going to be alright. We'd talk about her making better choices next time. Fuck it. There'd be no next time. She wouldn't be going to another fucking concert without me and she damn sure wouldn't be on the back of that mother fucker's bike again. Yeah, tomorrow we'd have a long talk.

Chapter Eleven

Reagan

Ugh. I rub my eyes trying to get the sleep out of them. I groan as I move. My whole body hurts. My tongue feels like sandpaper, my head is pounding, my pussy is sore, and my damn ass feels like it's on fire. What the hell happened last night?

I try to think. I open my eyes and glance around. I'm in Mason's bedroom. I look over and he's asleep with an arm thrown over his eyes. His other arm is on me. My gaze wanders down his body until it lands on the godzilla dick that's laying over his thigh. That's when it all comes rushing back. Avery had drugged me and I'd fucked Mason all night. But, wait? How did Mason find me so fast?

And, where had Avery disappeared to? Wait, I'd seen Avery before we left. We'd fought and then she was laying against the trash cans. My lips tremble and my eyes fill with tears when I realize why her head had been at an odd angle. Mason had killed her. Oh, God! I, slowly, get out of bed and head to the bathroom. I need to get out of here.

First, though, I need to shower. I smell like dirty sex and his fucking semen. I let the shower get as hot as it can before I step in the spray. The tears fall as I wash my hair and body. I let out a little laugh as I realize I've been here before with him. Is this ever going to work between us? God, I'm in love with an obsessive, psychotic murderer! What the fuck is wrong with me? With us? How the fuck did I even get to this point in my life?

I get out and rub myself dry with the towel before wrapping it around my body. I open the bathroom door as quietly as possible and step into the room. My eyes dart around looking for my clothes. I find them in the floor, torn apart. That's when I remember he'd ruined them while we were still at the concert. I feel tears roll down my cheeks. My ass and pussy ache with each step I take towards his dresser, a reminder of last night's events.

I pull out one of my tshirts and a pair of jeans that I'd left here. I slowly put them on because my body isn't allowing me to move any faster. I look at the nightstand where my phone is laying and hold my breath as I tiptoe towards it. As I'm reaching down to grab it, I feel a shift in the air. It's at that moment I know that he's awake and watching me. I try to act normal as I hit the home button and see that I've missed numerous calls and texts from my mom.

My brow furrows because she never calls me. I open the text and feel all the blood drain from my face. The cops are at my house wanting to talk to me about Avery. Fuck!

"What's wrong, Reagan? You look like you've just seen the boogeyman."

Oh, how right he is. I'm looking right at the boogeyman. Those green eyes are eating me up. Sorry buddy. The pussy shop is closed!

"I've got to get home." My voice is barely a whisper. My throat is killing me. I'm sure it's from choking on his dick. I close my eyes and feel the tears welling up as I think of all the dirty things we'd done last night. How could he have taken such advantage of me like that. He knew I didn't want to do anal! Bastard! Yes, I'd let him. But, I was fucking high! I wanted to scream. I wanted to fucking pound his face in.

I had to get out of here. I couldn't lose my shit right now. I had to think straight when dealing with Mason and the fucking cops. God, this was a fucking mess. And, all because he couldn't just let me live a little without him up my ass. No pun intended.

"How could you, Mason? How could you kill her?" The tears were flowing freely now. I felt the lump in my throat grow to where I could hardly breath. I watched as his eyes hardened and his nostrils flared.

"Because she fucking drugged you! She drugged you so that she could fuck you. She offered to let me watch and fuck you both, Reagan!"

A dry laugh escaped me. "How's that any different than what you did last night? You fucked me while I was high as a fucking kite!"

"Baby, we both know I'd be buried deep in that pussy whether you were high or not. It's probably wet for me now." His smirk as he spoke made my blood boil. It pissed me off even more that he was right. My pussy got wet the second he spoke.

"And what about my ass, Mason? You fucking knew I didn't want to do that!"

"Reagan, the third time you were begging me to fuck it. You loved every second of it. You came all over my dick! You were lapping cum off your titties with your tongue."

He stood up from the bed, his dick hard as a rock. I couldn't take my eyes off of him as he stroked it. I felt myself lick my lips, wishing they were wrapped around his dick. When he came closer I stepped away, shaking off the lustful spell he was weaving. I had to get away from him.

"I've got to go, Mason. The cops are at my house." he stopped mid stroke. His eyes turning hard again.

"What?" His voice deceptively low. I knew there was a storm brewing inside of him now. That's the way he worked.

"Mason, how do you think this is going to work? Am I supposed to just lay on back and fuck you whenever you want while you go around murdering everyone you deem unworthy? Is that how this works? How many people have you killed? How long have you been doing this shit because you were too calm with after the first one I witnessed for that to have been your first time?" My voice had gotten stronger with each word I spoke. I was going to get some fucking answers before I left.

"Do you want the truth, Reagan? Because there's no going back." The darkness was back in his voice. That evil that lurked beneath the surface was shining through. I felt myself tremble but nodded my head.

"I started killing whores when I was twelve, maybe thirteen. My father and his buddies would give me their leftovers." He pauses, licking his lips. "I remember my first one. She was this beautiful blonde with a set of the nicest tits I'd ever seen, until yours. God, yours make me so hard."

I feel vomit rising up in my throat listening to him. He talks about murder like he's ordering dinner at a restaurant. I feel myself shaking and turn to leave the room. He grabs me and pulls my body against his. His dick grinding against my ass. “I’m not letting you leave me, Reagan.” A chill rips down my spine at his words.

His lips start placing kisses up my neck to my ear. His teeth nip my earlobe. Tears stream down my cheeks. Oh God! I’ve been fucking a monster that’s been killing since his early teens.

“I have to go now, Mason. If I don’t they’ll be coming here.” I whisper and pray he’ll let me leave.

“Dad!!!” Mason yells and makes me jump. His hands rub up and down my arms. “I’ll never hurt you, Reagan and I’ll never let anyone else hurt you.”

Charles opens the bedroom door and averts his gaze to the ceiling when he realizes Mason is buck naked. His hands are still rubbing my arms. His father clears his throat. “What did you need, Mason?”

Mason kisses my cheek. “Reagan has to go home because the police are there waiting for her. I want you to call one of your lawyer friends and accompany her to her place.

She doesn't seem to want me there so I'm entrusting you to take care of her. Do we understand each other?"

Charles drills Mason with his eyes. "Why do the police want to talk to Reagan?"

I don't know what needs to be said so I stay quiet.

Mason shrugs behind me. "Apparently, one of her friends got killed last night at the concert they went to." How the hell did he say that so calmly knowing that he was the reason she was dead. I felt tears build up in my eyes again. Fuck! I didn't know if I could do this. How was I going to keep a straight face with the cops? I'd lied to cops before but never about something like this. God, I'd helped cover up his last murder, too! Or, I assumed it was his last murder. How the hell did I know there hadn't been more since then?

Taking a deep breath, I square my shoulders and walk away from Mason. This time he lets me go. I step around Charles and head down the stairs.

"What the fuck, Mason? What the fuck have you done this time? And put some goddamn pants on!"

I don't hear anymore as I fly down the rest of the stairs. I need air. I rush out the front door and sit on the steps outside. I grip my head in my hands and rock out and back. I've got to get a grip.

It's not long until I feel someone's hand touch my shoulder. "Reagan, let's go." It's Charles. Shit. Am I ready? Taking a deep breath, I stand up and head to his car. "The lawyer is meeting us there. I'm not sure bringing me or the lawyer is a good idea. It may make you appear guilty of something. However, it's what Mason wants and I think we both know a calm Mason is a safe Mason."

His hands grip the steering wheel so tight his knuckles turn white. I stay quiet the whole ride there. We pull into the trailer park and my heart immediately starts pounding. I feel hot and out of breath. There are two cop cars and a car I don't recognize in our little driveway. Charles pulls on the other side of our trailer out of the way.

"Stick to short answers and don't tell them anymore than what they ask. If you get nervous just tap your finger against your knee and I'll try to direct the conversation to give you time to calm down. Good, Calvin just pulled in. He'll stay quiet until we need him. Don't worry. You've done nothing wrong, so you're not in any trouble."

He gets out of the car and comes around to open my door. It's then I realize my feet are bare. I pray no one notices.

We reach the front door and it swings open. An officer stares at each of us before letting us pass through. My mom is sitting on the couch smoking. Her face is pale. There's a total of three cops and a couple sitting at the small kitchen table. I recognize them as Avery's parents. I've seen their pics on her facebook. Fuck!

They both give me a look of disgust before their gaze falls to Charles behind me. I go and sit beside my mom. Her hand goes to my back. She gives me an awkward pat before returning to her cigarette.

Officer Briggs stands in front of me, staring me down before he starts in. "Reagan, can you tell us where you've been and where you were yesterday afternoon?"

"I was at my boyfriend's house, why?" I'm so proud that my voice sounded so calm.

"So, you were at your boyfriend's house all of yesterday and this morning?" He cocks his head to the side, studying me. It almost reminds me of Mason when he's trying to get inside my head.

"No, sir." Keep my answers short. That's what Charles had said.

The officer sighs. "No to what, Reagan?"

"No, I wasn't at his house all of yesterday."

He sighs even louder. "Okay, Reagan. Let's try this. Where all did you go yesterday after school?" He sounds agitated. Well, get in line buddy. I'm pretty fucking agitated as well.

"I came home, took a shower, got dressed, went to a concert, and fell asleep at my boyfriend's house." There. I didn't go into detail and gave him all honest answers. I was very fucking proud of myself.

He grabs his gun belt and looks towards the other officers. "Did you go to the concert alone?" His gaze swings back to me.

"Yes."

“Really? That’s interesting because we have it on good authority that you went with Avery Mitchell.”

Fuck. “No, I didn’t. I met up with her there.”

“You met up with her? Okay, when did you last see her?”

“We hang out and listened to a few of the bands. I went to get another drink when I ran into Mason. Then, we left. Why are you asking me about Avery?” Fuck! I should’ve just said I last saw her when I was leaving.

“So, you just left your friend there?” He sounds so condescending.

“What was I supposed to do? She came by herself just like I did. We weren’t planning to leave together. I was ready to go, so I left. I don’t understand what the big deal is?”

“Avery was found dead last night, Reagan. Her neck was broken and she was left beside the dumpster. Is that what you thought of your friend, Reagan? DId you just kill her and leave her with the trash?” I feel my lips tremble. My eyes fill with tears. God!

"I didn't know. I didn't know Avery was dead." My voice is barely above a whisper. I don't even know if they heard me. I hear her parents crying.

"I think that's enough questions for now. Unless you are planning to arrest Reagan, I suggest you all leave."

Officer Briggs ignores the lawyer and squats down so that he's eye level with me. "I saw the pictures on Avery's phone, Reagan. I also saw the video. Does your boyfriend know you were fucking Avery? Does he know about your little threesome you had going on with her and the vp of local MC?"

I push my fingers to my eyes. Oh my God! She had recorded us? Fuck! And what pictures were on her phone?

"That's enough, Officer. No more questions. Reagan, don't say another word."

The other two officers step outside. Officer Briggs stays where he's at staring at me. I see a hint of lust in his eyes before he hides it. "We'll be in touch, Reagan. This isn't finished."

He steps to the door and waits on her parents to follow. Her mother stops before leaving. Her glare directed at me. "I can't believe my Avery would ever touch a piece of trash like you. I swear I'll see you fry, you stupid slut!"

Her husband nudges her and follows her out. When they all leave, I lean back against the couch and close my eyes. This was a fucking mess and the culprit wasn't even here!

"Obviously, they have no evidence or they would've hauled her in. So, just keep your story straight. If you need me, just call anytime Charles." He shakes hands and leaves. Charles pulls a chair from the kitchen and straddles it, propping his arms over the back.

"Okay, Cindy. This is how this is going to go. You're going to say and do whatever I tell you. Your daughter is going to stick to her story. If anyone has any questions or problems they're going to contact me and I'll reach out to Calvin. Now, is there anything anyone would like to discuss before I head home?"

I just lean back again and close my eyes.

"Yeah, who the fuck are you and how the fuck do you know my name?" My mom's voice is raspy from all the cigarettes she's inhaled over the years. I have to smile at her attitude. She's a feisty old bitch.

I peek at Charles to see how he's handling her disrespect. He smirks at her. "I check out all the sluts my son fucks." He gives my mom a once over. "I also check out their slutty mothers."

My mom flips him the bird and lights up another cigarette. "Now, unless, you have anything of interest to add, I'm going home." With that he gets up and slams out of the trailer.

"Does Mason let him talk to you like that?" I open my eyes to see mom staring at me with interest.

"Nope."

"You going to tell him what he just said?"

"Nope."

"Why not?"

"Because he'd probably kill him." I sigh. My mom nods and turns away. "I'm going to lay down for a bit. If anyone asks, I'm not here."

"I'll try to hold him off." We both know he'll come for me. I just hope I can at least get some rest first. I walk to my room and strip off my clothes. I snuggle under my covers, my body still aches from last night's activities. I wouldn't dare admit it to Mason but, I do remember him fucking my ass and how good it felt. Honestly, I'd let him do it again. However, I'm going to fight against it on principal. He knew I hadn't wanted to go that far, yet. He'd done it anyway while I was high and unable to refuse.

I knew he'd never let me go. He'd hunt me down and drag me back like the last time I'd ran from him. But, he'd let me set up some rules after that. I was going to do that again. I feared him and the things he seemed to have no problem doing. So, I was going to add more boundaries. If he didn't agree then maybe I could somehow convince him to set me free.

I sighed. Who the hell I was kidding? I was in love with the lunatic. We were both damned to hell. I could've just told the cops what happened last night. Although, I didn't know all the specifics because I was pretty fucked up. It would've been enough to lock his ass up and I hadn't done it.

I feel my eyes getting heavy and welcome the escape from reality. My last thoughts before drifting off... Would I ever be able to tame Mason? A scarier thought was, did I want to?

Chapter Twelve

“Let’s cut through the bullshit, Cindy. We both fucking know she is in here and that I’m not fucking leaving till I get to see her.”

“I told you. She left right after your father did.” I had to give it to my mom. Her voice didn’t waver as she spoke that lie. I was also surprised she was standing up to him. She was terrified of him even when he wasn’t in her presence.

Sighing, I throw the covers back and get out of bed. I don’t even bother with clothes as I walk to the living room. I’m taking a page from Mason’s book. I’ll use my nudity to distract him from terrorizing my mother.

As soon as I step in the room, his nostrils flare and his eyes dilate. Oh yeah, at this moment I hold all the power. Without another word, I turn back to my room knowing that he’ll follow. I put an extra sway to my hips when I feel him. I crawl back in bed, facing the wall. The sound of clothes rustling tells me that he's undressing.

The bed shifts with his weight, his heat at my back. "Why are you hiding from me, Reagan?" His fingers trail my spine and stop at my butt cheeks. He palms my cheeks, squeezing each one. "Are you still sore, Reagan?" He grips my bottom. "Please tell me you're not."

"I'm not hiding, Mason. I just wanted to get some sleep." I push my ass against him until I'm rubbing against his erection. "And yes, I'm still fucking sore."

He groans and grinds his dick against me until it's sliding between my cheeks. I tense and try to pull away but he holds me steady. "Oh no you don't, you little cocktease." His mouth latches onto my neck, biting and sucking. "Mmmm, you want to play, Reagan?" His hand goes between my legs, sliding through my wet folds. I bite my lip to hold back my moan. Why does my body always ache for him?

"That's right, baby. This pussy always remembers who it belongs to. It's always wet and ready for me." His words make my clit throb. His fingers circle it, teasing, before lightly pinching it. I jerk in response. My nipples tighten, making my breasts ache to be touched.

I close my eyes and shudder, remembering him titty fucking me last night. God! I moan and push back against him. Then, I remember the deal I made with myself before falling asleep this morning.

I flip over to face him. I grab his face with both of my hands as his hand continues stroking my pussy. One of his fingers eases inside almost distracting me from my mission. “Wait, Mason. I have to talk to you about something.”

He wiggles his finger, stroking against my g-spot, making me whimper. Oh, God! “Please, Mason. Let me say this and then you can fuck me.” I lower my voice and lick his lips slowly. “I’ll let you fuck me any way you want to.”

I watch his eyes darken as my words sink in. His finger slides out of my pussy and eases its way towards my ass. “You want me to fuck your ass, baby?” I moan as he pushes his wet finger into my ass. It burns but I make myself relax. I push my tongue into his mouth and rub my pussy against his dick. He groans in my mouth and I pull away.

"I want you to fuck me however you want, Mason." I rub my tits against his chest. His finger starts thrusting in and out of my ass. It hurts at first but then it starts to feel nice. I feel my pussy growing even more wet. Oh, God. Was I going to come like this? I know I did last night but I'd been on ecstasy.

"Mason." I feel my body explode, my thighs are wet with my orgasm. I open my eyes and see Mason breathing hard, licking his lips, and staring at me in awe.

He raises up and moves over me, rubbing his dick against my clit. I clamp my legs shut before he can make his move. "We're talking first."

He lets out a breath before settling himself over me, putting his weight on his elbows. His hands rubbing my face. "What is it, Reagan?"

I grip his biceps and take a breath. My heart is racing in my chest, my pussy pulsing, and I'm still trembling from my orgasm. "All we do is fuck, Mason. That's all our relationship is. We never go on dates. We never do anything but school and fuck. I want more." I wait, holding my breath.

"You want me to take you on a date, Reagan?" He smiles down at me. I can't decide if he's being genuine or laughing at me.

"I'm serious, Mason. If you want to be with me, we're going to do more than fuck." I shudder when I feel his dick slide between my clenched thighs. They're so soaked from my orgasm that he glided right through. He groans. "That feels so fucking good. I'm so hard for you, Reagan. I could come right now without even being in that sweet pussy." He keeps moving his hips between my legs.

I feel myself inching them open, trying to get him to rub against my pussy. My hands stroke up his biceps until they rest on his shoulders. I pull his head down to my mouth. "Please, Mason."

His tongue licks against my lips. "Please, what? Fuck you or take you out?"

I moan as he pushes his dick against my entrance. "Both." Something else enters my mind suddenly. Before he can enter me, I reach down and grip his dick. He groans. "Baby."

"One other thing." The seriousness in my voice makes him open his eyes. "No more killing!"

He lets out his breath and rolls off of me. He throws an arm over his face. What the hell?

I climb on top of him, straddling his waist. His dick is still hard. I grab it, easing it inside me. I lean back, using his thighs to balance myself. I glide up and down. I watch his chest rise up and down, faster and faster. It's not long until I see his eyes peeking out to watch my tits bounce up and down. I know he loves my tits. "Mason, look at me."

He closes his eyes again, shifting his arm to keep them from my view. Okay, then. I ease off him and decide to try something different. I reach over to my night stand and grab my dildo. It's bright purple with a clit stimulator attached. I lay beside Mason and turn it on. I rub it through my slit until it's wet, gliding it inside my pussy. It's nothing like Mason's dick but with the clit stimulation it'll get me off in no time.

I amp up the speed and let it fuck me. I moan and pinch my nipple. When I feel him watching me, I lift my breast to my mouth and lick my nipple. He growls low in his throat before he jerks my dildo out of me and throws it across the room.

"The only dick you're allowed to fuck is mine." He grabs my thighs pulling me to him. His dick slides inside me, stretching me to my limit. I moan, loving it. He growls again before reaching down to suck a nipple in his mouth. I throw my head back in ecstasy as his hips start pistoning in and out.

"You like that, Reagan?" He leans down to my ear, licking the shell. "You like my dick in you, fucking you? Hmmm, baby?" He picks up speed, breathing hard in my ear. I feel my walls clamp down on his dick as my orgasm tears through me. Tears leave my eyes as I whimper. "That's it, baby. Come all over my dick."

He pulls out as the last of my tremors rush through my body. He crawls up my body, his dick rubbing my juices all over my lips. "Taste yourself, Reagan. Taste that sweet pussy." I moan as my tongue laps up my orgasm from his dick. When I suck the head of his dick into my mouth, his hands fist my hair, making my thighs clench.

I suck him in deep, running my tongue beneath the crown. I pop his dick from my mouth, gripping the base as I suck his balls in my mouth. He throws his head back and groans. I run my tongue up the base and swirl it around the head. "I want more, Mason. I want you to fuck me again, please." I whimper and tongue the slit of his cock. His cum leaks out and I lap it up.

He pulls back and flips me over. "Ass up, baby." I feel him rub his dick against my ass and tense up. I know I'd promised him any way he wanted it, but I was still sore from our previous sex fest. I didn't know if I could handle it this soon. But, he surprised me by sliding into my pussy. I gripped the sheets, moaning and pushing myself against him. My walls clenched around him, his answering groan made me even shudder.

As my orgasm washed over me, a thought entered my mind. What kind of nasty bitch was I? How was I any better than Mason? I'm laying here letting him fuck my brains out after discovering the fact that he broke my friend's neck last night like it was nothing… After him confessing to murdering

God knows how many women over the years… After watching him kill my mom's boyfriend! Who the fuck was I?

Fear suddenly gripped me so hard that I could barely breathe. I jerked away from Mason and scrambled off the bed so fast, I tripped and hit the floor. "What the fuck are you doing, Reagan?" He moves to get off the bed and come towards me, but I hold my hand up.

"Don't, please." I take deep breaths trying to calm my heart. It's currently trying to beat it's way out of my chest. Oh, God. Tears stream down my face, my whole body is trembling, and my stomach is twisting. I feel vomit rising up and rush to the bathroom. I spill the contents of my stomach into the porcelain bowl, heaving over and over until my ribs feel like they're cracked.

When I can breathe again, I rise up and brush my teeth. I run a cool washcloth over my face and stare at the stranger in the mirror. I don't know her anymore. The girl in the mirror is not me. Or is it?

I enter my bedroom and see Mason sitting on the side of the bed fully dressed. His head is gripped in his hands. He doesn't look up as I enter, just keeps holding his head with it directed towards the floor. I wrap my arms around my my naked torso not knowing what else to do.

"I don't know what to do, Reagan. I don't know what you want from me. I can't give you what you want. I thought love meant no matter what. I thought it meant you'd love me no matter my faults or what I'd done. But, it doesn't. It means that as long as I'm what you want me to be that you'll love me, right? Well, I can't give you that. So, the question is do you still want to fucking be with me?"

His piercing green eyes finally look up at me. They seem to see right through me before raking down my body. His nostrils flare before he stands up. He moves towards me, stopping inches away. "I'll give you the rest of the day to think about us and what the fuck you want."

I slide down the wall and hit my ass hard on the floor when he leaves my room. My hands shake as I bring them to my face, wiping away the tears. We were explosive together but at the same time our relationship seemed to shred me more than make me stronger. A part of me knew that even if I told him I didn't want him anymore, he wouldn't just let me walk away. He'd proven that when he'd busted in the MC's clubhouse. He'd taken on a whole gang of bikers to get to me.

So, that left me two options. Either stay with Mason or run for my life. I decided sleep was what I needed. Sleep the day away and however I felt when I awoke would be how I made my decision. Run or Stay.

Chapter Thirteen

Mason

I didn't drive home after leaving my heart behind in that room. Instead, I'd parked my truck in the vacant lot two trailers down from her. I'd stayed in my fucking truck all afternoon and all night to make sure she didn't bail on me.

Fuck! Why had I let her get so far beneath my skin? Why had I given her my heart so fucking freely? I left just after eight this morning to see if she was going to make an escape. There was no movement so I felt it would be safe to come home, shower, and change clothes. I punch the wall heading up the stairs and hear a picture fall, bounce against the steps before shattering on the floor. I don't even turn around. Moaning and groaning echo around me as I reach the top. Dad's got a fucking orgy going on in his study.

I pause at my bedroom door. I'm at war with myself. It feels like something is inside my skull trying to claw its way out. Fuck! I step away from my door and swing open the one to the study. My father and his friends are fucking two beautiful sluts. A blonde and a redhead. The redhead pulls Frank's dick out of her mouth long enough to look me up and down, licking her lips.

I smirk back at her. Careful what you wish for, beautiful. "I want the redhead when y'all are through." My father's head swings my way. A frown mars his brow as he looks at me, stopping mid thrust.

"Where's Reagan?" The blonde protests when he stops, which results in her getting a hard smack on her ass.

"Not here." With that I turn back towards my room. I lay on my bed til I hear a light knock. I didn't shower. I want the bitch to taste Reagan's pussy on my dick.

"Come in." The redhead comes in with a seductive sway to her hips. I stand up, unzipping my jeans. When I pull my dick out, I see her eyes widen and watch as she licks her lips in appreciation. "Get on your knees, bitch."

She complies and I grip her hair as I ram my dick down her throat. Her hands grip my thighs trying to push me away to gain relief. Too bad that wasn't going to happen. I was amped up and pissed. I couldn't punish the one I wanted to, so she'd have to do. I continued thrusting in and out of her mouth. I loved watching the tears streak her cheeks and the slobber go down her chin as she gagged on my dick.

She gurgled as she tried to beg me to stop but couldn't speak since I refused to let her have an ounce of relief. Like I said, sweetheart, careful what you wish for. The beast was out and I was giving him free range.

I felt my balls tighten and decided it was time for the finale. "Get up on the bed. I want you on all fours." Her legs shook as she stood. I saw the trepidation in her eyes. I went to the nightstand and pulled out a condom. I rolled it on and grabbed my belt from the floor. I stepped behind and brought my belt down as hard as I could on her ass. Her screams echoed around the room over and over as I continued lashing her with my belt.

When her ass was beautifully red and marks from the belt were rising up, I positioned my dick at her recently used ass. I shoved inside her without seeing if she was still lubed. She tried to jerk away but it was too late. I was in her ass as far as I could go. She began to cry I pumped in and out of her.

I reached around and stroked her clit, deciding to give her one last orgasm before she took her last breath. She let up on her crying to give a sigh. I pinched down on her clit and felt her climax spray my balls. Her head turned to the side to watch my face, her pupils were dilated and she looked high.

I grabbed my belt and looped it around her neck. She started to struggle against me when I tightened it. I groaned as her ass tightened around my dick when she began fighting me. I jerked the belt hard, almost snapping her neck. It seemed to daze her as she went limp for a minute. I pulled hard, choking her as my thrusts grew more frantic. Sweat beaded my forehead and some ran down my spine.

I looked down at my dick and saw some blood coating it where I had thrust into her dry. That just amped up my pleasure. Fuck, I was about to come before watching her die.

Pulling out of her, I ripped the condom off with one hand while using the other to continue choking her. This wasn't going fast enough. Her face was turning a beautiful shade of purple. I used both my hands to pull harder. Her hands were clawing at the belt, trying to give herself relief.

Her hands started going limp, her body began to sag, and I knew she was there. She was on the precipice between life and death. Her head began to lull and I jerked her head to the side to watch the life leave her eyes. THey began to glaze over and I groaned. Her mouth went slack, drool coming out the sides. I watched her whole body shudder as she died. I let her go and stroked myself until jets of semen lashed against those gorgeous welts I'd put on her ass.

When I was finished, I stood there catching my breath before flipping her over to remove the belt. I felt myself get hard again as I took in the bruised necklace I'd left her with. My gaze raked down to her tits. They were fake but still fucking nice. Her pussy was cleanly shaven and a sweet shade of pink.

I should've fucked it, too.

I froze when I sensed I wasn't the only one in the room. I turned my head slightly and saw Reagan standing in the doorway, her mouth covered with her hand, tears streak her cheeks. I rush her before her fight or flight instincts kick in. I crush her mouth with mine, my tongue thrusting into her mouth. I grunt when she bites down on my tongue, the coppery taste of blood coating our mouths.

I pull away, kissing up her throat and tracing the shell of her ear with my tongue. "How much did you watch, baby? Did you watch the beautiful way she died? Did it make that tight little pussy wet for me?"

I feel her shudder against me and weep harder. I have to know. She'll lie to me and I want to know. I push my hand inside the waistband of her jeans and slide a finger through her soaked slit. My cock throbs against her jeans, I feel cum seeping from the head. Fuck. It fucking turned her on watching me fuck and kill that whore.

"Oh, Reagan." I drop my forehead against hers. I continue stroking her pussy. Her breathing picks up pace.

"What's wrong with me, Mason?" Her voice sounds pained. She grips the back of my neck, her nails digging in my skin. "What the fuck have you done to me?" She shoves me back hard. THe only reason my body moves is because I allow it. Her strength is no match for mine. I even stand there and allow her to slap the shit out of my face. My cheeks stings and I grit my teeth to keep from retaliating.

"You fucked her! I watched you fuck her!" She slaps me again and again. Before the fourth slap lands, I grip her wrist.

"That's enough." I feel the darkness still clawing at my skull. But, I'll never allow it to touch her. Never. I"ll kill myself first. "And, going by the moisture on my fingers…" I lean down to her ear and whisper, "you fucking loved, you dirty girl."

Her hands fist at her sides. I watch her breasts heave up and down with her rapid breathing. "No, I didn't. I wanted to kill you both, Mason. I wanted to slit her fucking throat for touching your dick. I thought it was mine. I thought you were mine! How would you feel if you walked in on my riding Devil's dick?"

I can't stop myself from shoving her against the wall. I grip her hips, pushing her body up until my cock aligns with her slit. I rub myself against the denim of her jeans. "The only dick you'll be riding is mine." I growl against her throat before I nip the sensitive skin.

"But, I won't be the only pussy you'll be fucking?" Her voice a soft whimper. Her eyes look up at me as though I just shattered her world. My heart cracks a little. I know I fucked up but she caused it by questioning us.

"I didn't fuck her pussy, Reagan. I fucked her mouth and ass. Then, I really rocked her world. But, guess what? She's fucking dead. She'll never remember how good I felt. But, you will. You'll always know and remember. This is the only way I can keep it under control. I need this outlet to keep you safe. It's either that or my own death. You choose."

I close my against the cry that leaves her throat. She grips me against her and I hold her as she cries herself out. I have to wonder why this beautiful creature even wants me? I don't have an answer to that. I just know that I'll never let her go.

I do know the image of her fucking Devil shredded me. He's been a thorn in my side ever since I clapped eyes on that mother fucking tattoo. He had to go. It would have to wait, though. It'd have to be done in a clever way. I didn't want her to suspect me and I didn't want to lead the MC to my door. Although, I'd take them all on for this girl. I'd slay the mother fucking world to make her happy.

"What made you wet, Reagan? Hmmm... What turned that tight pussy on?" I kiss the sides of her mouth before tracing the seam of her lips with my tongue.

Her legs tighten around my waist and I feel her nipples harden. Fuck!

"Watching you choke her. Watching you come all over her ass made me want to kill her again. I don't know what's fucking wrong with me. I wanted to be there on my knees catching every drop of it in my mouth. I pictured that in my head as I watched you. I'm so fucked up, Mason. I'm as fucked up as you are. What the hell is wrong with me?"

I cup her face and smash our mouths together, our teeth hitting. My tongue sweeps inside claiming her. My hands glide down her sides, as I go to work unbuttoning her jeans and sliding the zipper down. I ease her legs down, so I can remove the denim keeping me from her.

She whimpers as I pull my mouth away. I decide to test the darkness that seems to be seeping it's way inside her. After pulling her shirt off her, I pick her back up. My eyes don't leave her tits as they bounce from the movement. My mouth latches onto a nipple and she throws her head back, moaning. That's it baby, give in to it.

I put her down and turn her around to face the dead whore on my bed. She tenses up until my hand reaches between her legs to stroke her clit. "Look at her, Reagan. Look at that pretty necklace I gifted her with." She soaks my hand and her body trembles. I crouch down and lick those slick folds. She moans and pushes against my face. I sink two fingers in her pussy and groan when that greedy pussy squeezes against them.

When she comes on my face, I can't take anymore. I have to be inside her. I thrust into her hard. I look down and watch my dick sink inside that tight pussy. My gaze makes its way up to her other tight hole. I want back in that ass but I'll wait.

"Look at her, Reagan. Does her death turn you on, baby?" My hips swivel, stretching her. She screams as she comes again. I pull out of her before I find my own climax. "Get on your knees, baby." She turns around and opens her mouth for me. Her eyes glitter up at me. I stroke myself, my cum jetting in her mouth and on her face. When I'm done, she grabs my dick, sucking it into her hot little mouth. I grunt as I watch her suck me clean. She releases me, licking her lips.

Chapter Fourteen

I know the moment when what we just done sinks in. Her eyes seem to dull and her hands begin to shake. I put my finger under her chin making her look up at me. "Nothing is wrong with us. Everyone has their quirks. Ours is just a little different, okay? I could show you so many videos of worse things. Do you hear me?" She nods slowly but I know she's still not okay.

"Get dressed while I get someone to get her ass out of here." I stand in the doorway, waiting until she's out of the room. When she's shut the bathroom door behind her, I let out a piercing whistle. My dad, Frank, and Dave all three step out of the study and head towards me. They know the drill. I smirk as they all step in my room and take in the scene before them.

They all tense when the bathroom door opens and Reagan steps out. I let out a growl when I see her nipples poking through her shirt. I know these sick fucks notice. A part of me loves that she never gives a fuck what others think of her and another part of me hates that she freely shows off her body.

My father shoots me a smirk, knowing what sets me off. That's okay, pops. I'll fuck you up later. My spine stiffens when he shoots off his mouth.

"What the fuck were you thinking letting her witness this shit?" Dear old Dad still has balls. I'll give him that. Frank and Dave are too afraid of me to question me. I know Dad fears me but he also knows I require his finesse with these little clean ups.

My eyes go to Reagan. I find a smile when she glares at my father. She's got fucking spunk. My love for her grows when she steps forward, her shoulders thrown back, that head cocked to the side, and chin lifted. "Who the fuck do you think whipped her?" Her voice never wavered and I find myself almost busting out of my jeans.

I have to adjust to give my cock relief. She watches, licking her lips. Later, baby. You can have it all, later.

All three men stare at her like she's grown a second head and I almost laugh. "Just get her the fuck out here before you all end up laying next to her. Come on, Reagan. It's time for that date." She walks around them, her head held high. When she laced her fingers through mine, my heart seems to skip a beat.

We get in my truck. She finds my hand again, holding it in hers before she starts playing with the radio. She settles on a station and sits back. I don't really know what to say to her because I can't figure out if she was just covering for me back there or if she's really fine with what took place.

I pull up to the movie theater that resides in the next town from ours. I don't really want to run into anyone we know. I want to cherish this day with my girl. She picks some horror film and I buy the tickets. We move to the concession line. She grabs a box of bunch of crunch and a cherry coke icee. I can't help but smile when I watch her take a sip. She could bring me to knees if she wanted. Hell, she had not long ago with my face buried in her pussy.

I throw my arm over her shoulder and come to a stop as she seems to freeze. My spine stiffens as I search for the source of her tension. That's when I see them. Devil and a few of his crew are waiting in line to get inside the movie. His eyes rake her body up and down. Fury surges through me but I keep it under control. His time is coming, he just doesn't know it. I pull her with me to get in line behind them.

One of his crew turns towards us smiling. "Looking good, Reagan. I miss seeing you around the club."

She smiles back but doesn't reply. When the douchebag looks towards me he just smirks. I'll fuck you up, too, buddy. I smirk back and let the darkness creep it's way into my gaze. I watch as he falters when he sees my true self. I know how chilling my gaze is, I've seen it in the mirror.

Reagan looks up at me and bumps me with her hip. "Behave." I tear my gaze away and gaze down upon this angel attached to my side. She somehow calmed the savage beast that lurked just beneath the surface. I leaned down and brushed my lips against hers teasingly. I kept up the tender assault until I heard her little whimper. She was being tortured by my teasing. I licked against her lips until she opened for me.

She dropped the box of candy as she gripped my shirt for support as I ravaged her mouth. I pulled back, lightly kissing her mouth before turning towards our audience. Anger and jealousy was shining through Devil's eyes. That's right, fucker. I owned her. Body and soul. I bent down and picked up Reagan's candy. She smiled as I handed it to her. Her hand was trembling. "I'll finish that later." She shuddered as I whispered in her ear.

The line finally started moving so we could get settled in the theater. She picked seats towards the middle. I wasn't a fan of movies but she had asked for us to start doing things together that didn't involve fucking. I'd give her whatever she wanted as long as she stayed with me. Well, almost anything. I tried to get into the movie but the story line was so fucking obvious. Reagan jumped a few times and grabbed my bicep. I smiled and put my arm around her shoulders.

When the credits finally lit the screen, I let out a sigh of relief. I decided I would take her out for dinner before heading home to fuck her brains out. We were at my truck, I'd just opened the door when I felt them behind me. They just couldn't let us be. "Mason, don't." I heard Reagan whisper. But, they were challenging me. I wouldn't back down.

"My gun is in the dash, Reagan. If you need it, it's there." I keep my voice low, so they don't hear me. I squeeze her thigh before turning to face them. I'm not surprised when the barrel of a glock is pushed against my forehead.

"Well, where's your rich daddy and the cop on your payroll, now? Did you think you could actually break into my club and steal my girl with no repercussions, rich boy?" Devil's ice blue eyes full of hatred clashed against mine.

"That's funny because if memory serves me. I popped the cherry in that pussy. So, that means that pussy was never yours and neither was she. Now, fuck off before I fuck you up." I grinned when I saw the jealousy light up his features. I knew he was going to strike me when his body shifted. I was going to get beat down because there was too many of them but I would give it back to them as long as I could.

I caught his forearm when he went to hit me with his gun. Fucking pussy. I would've blown his brains out if the roles were reversed. I hit him with a right to his chin and came back with a left as I released his arm. He staggered for a minute before trying to knock me back with the weight of his body. I twisted to the side and watched as he stumbled. He was fighting with anger and getting sloppy.

It wasn't long before his buddies realized this wasn't going to go in his favor, so they surged forward getting in blows. I was hitting back but they were getting in more shots than I was giving. The douchebag from earlier was about to deliver a kick to my ribs when I fell to my knees from a punch to the back of my head, but a shot rang out over us and we all froze. Reagan stood there, tears ran down her face, and the hands gripping the pistol shook. "Get the fuck away from him."

They all watched her before stepping away. Douchebag went to kick me anyway but another shot rang out making him drop. He screamed in agony, grabbing his knee. She'd shot his knee. Holy shit!

I stood, rushing towards her. We had to get out of here. Someone was going to call the cops after hearing gunshots. I looked over the theater to make sure there weren't' any security cameras. I let out my breath when there were none to be found. I threw her over my shoulder and tossed her back in the truck. Running around to my side, I started it and peeled out of the parking lot.

When I glanced her way, she was staring down at the gun in shock. I reached over and plucked it from her grip. Placing back in the dash, I grabbed her hand and kissed her knuckles. “It’s going to be okay, Reagan. You did the right thing.”

“They just kept hitting you. I couldn’t take it.” Her voice was shaky.

“I know, baby.”

I rubbed her hand while I drove. I decided dinner out was probably not a good idea. So, I hit a drive thru and ordered us burgers and fries. I handed her the bag after I dug mine out. I ate mine in a few bites and looked her way. She hadn’t touched her food.

“Reagan, you need to eat.” She slowly reached in and seemed to be in auto pilot. She ate slowly and said nothing. She ate half the burger before throwing the rest back in the bag. I didn’t say anything else. At least she’d eaten something.

When we pulled up at my house, I came around and helped her out of the truck.

Chapter Fifteen

My father was waiting for us when we entered. He was sitting on the bottom step with his glass of scotch. I watched as he swirled the liquid around in the glass before tossing back. When he'd swallowed, he looked us over. "We need to talk."

"Not now, old man."

"I wasn't asking, Mason." He stood and held my gaze.

"Just spill it." God, I didn't have time for this shit. I wanted to get her upstairs and help her relax. I felt like she was on the verge of freaking the fuck out.

"It's got to stop, Mason. I can't keep cleaning up after you."

I let out a dark laugh. "You know the score, Charles. And, you'll do whatever the fuck I want. I've got shit on all three of you. So, you keep me happy and you stay happy." I pushed passed him with Reagan behind me.

"There was a message left on my phone, Mason. They're coming for her." I stopped in my tracks.

"They'll have to kill me first." I felt the rage crashing over me. They fucking thought they could take her from me?

"I don't think they have a problem with that, son. I think that's the idea. Unless they decide to torture you with what they do to her first."

Reagan spoke behind me. "Devil wouldn't hurt me."

"Baby, you just shot a member of his crew. The rules of the club have to be met."

"What?" Charles shouted and shot a glare towards Reagan.

"Don't fucking look at her. I told you already, old man. Now, how about we turn the tables on them. You're going to call the sheriff and plant a few seeds in his head. Remind them about that video you said they watched on Avery's phone. Devil was in it and then let him listen to the message on your phone. He threatened Reagan. But, make it like he was threatening her because she knew he'd killed Avery. He was at the concert, too. She fucking rode with him there." The memory of her pressed against his back on his bike spiked my fury.

I wanted to cut his dick off and shove it down his throat for him to choke to death on.

"Mason, do you know what you are setting in motion? Do you know what clubs like that do to rats?" Charles seemed scared.

I give him my most chilling smile. "Do I look like I give a fuck? Devil will be getting fucked up the ass in prison while I'm fucking Reagan in the ass in my bedroom. It's a win win for me." I come down a few steps so that I'm face to face with him. "Besides, how the fuck will he know we ratted him out. They don't have to tell him anyone said shit. We can say they had our phones tapped since they're already investigating Reagan."

I get even closer and he takes a step back. "Unless, you're planning on snitching out your own flesh and blood, Dad?"

He shakes his head at me. “I’ll make the call.” I watch him a moment before nodding. I turn back towards Reagan and see she’s staring at me like she doesn’t know who the fuck I am.

I grab her hand and pull her along behind me. When we get to my room she pulls away from me and sits on the edge of my bed. “What are you doing? They’ll kill us if they find out you just set that in motion!”

I crouch down in front of her, wrapping my arms around her hips. “They’re never going to know, Reagan.”

She just shakes her head. I grip her chin. “Trust me, Reagan. Just trust me. I’ll always protect you.”

She takes a shuddering breath. “Seems like I was protecting you earlier.” I let out a chuckle. She was right.

“That’s because you’re my ride or die. We watch each other’s backs.”

She grabs my shoulders, pulling me in close. “I’m scared, Mason.” I love that’s she’s clinging to me but I hate the fear that’s consuming her. “I’m just so scared that we’re going to be ripped away from each other.”

"Nothing is going to happen to you. I promise."

I decide she just needs to rest. I pull her up and help her out of her clothes. I shrug my shirt and jeans off, deciding to keep my boxers on so that I don't fuck her. When I pull her body against mine and throw the covers over us, she lets out a little sigh. It's not long until I hear her breathing even out and know that she's asleep. I kiss the top of my head and squeeze her one last time before I close my eyes.

I come awake with a sinking feeling. My arm reaches out for Reagan, but she's not there. I open my eyes and see she's nowhere in my room. I raise up and hit the bathroom. I take my morning piss and think. I doubt she'd be downstairs with my dad. They did not like each other. I don't even know if she's ever spoken a word to my mom. Surely, she didn't go home after Devil's threat. Fuck!

I throw on clothes and run downstairs. I stop in the kitchen when I see my dad at the breakfast bar. He puts down his paper when he sees me. "It's done. They're supposed to hit the clubhouse after lunch today."

I nod. "Have you seen Reagan?" He takes a sip of his coffee and waits a beat before answering.

"She left about an hour ago. She said she wanted to shower and change clothes."

Anger engulfs me. "You just fucking let her leave? They threatened her life! How the fuck could you just let her leave?"

He shrugs. "I'm not supposed to look, touch, or even breath in her direction, remember?" That fucking sets me off.

"If a fucking hair on her head is out of place when I get her, I'm fucking you up!"

I rush to my truck and do seventy on my way to her place. Fuck! I slam my fist against the steering wheel over and over.

I barely put it in park as I pull up and jump out. I swing the door open and my stomach drops. Her mom is on the couch crying as she holds a note in her hand. Somehow, I know she's gone. I drop to my knees. She's fucking gone! Her mom stands and heads towards me with the note. I reach out a shaking hand to take it.

Mason,

Looking back on us, I see that I should've never let our relationship escalate as quickly as it did. I should've set up boundaries early on. God, what have I done to us? It's my fault. I take full responsibility. I just never realized that we were headed down the path we were and going to fall so fast and deep.

I'm so sorry that this all happened. I just want you to know that,no matter what happens, I'll always love you. You'll always hold a very special place in my heart. Please don't try to find me. I'm doing what is best for the both of us. We are too volatile together. Together, I fear we'll lose ourselves and become this massive tornado destroying everything in our path.

Before you do anything that you'll later regret, hear my words. Let me go… Just let me go, Mason.

Love Always,

Reagan

Let her go? What the fuck? That's like asking me to rip my heart out of my fucking chest and keep on living. I close my eyes and take some deep breaths. I wasn't ever going to let her just fucking walk away from me, from us. We were meant for each other!

I scan over the letter again and that's when a little detail catches my eye. There are devil horns over her name. Fuck! They'd taken her. They took my fucking girl! I'd kill them all. I'd torch their fucking clubhouse and slaughter them all…

Charles

I enter the Richland Institute, signing the form and showing my identification. The nurse behind the counter hands me my badge and buzzes me through the doors. I hate the stench of places like this. They reek of bleach, urine, and death.

I go down a few more hallways and get buzzed through three more doors before I make it to the room I want. Opening the door, I enter the light pink room. That was Isabella's favorite color. There were a dozen pink roses on the table beside her bed. They had her sitting in the chair by the window.

I sat down in the adjacent chair and picked up her hand. I slowly rubbed my thumb across her fingers. She's dressed in a pair of pink pajamas.

"I've missed you, sweetheart. Have you missed me?" Her eyes never leave the window. I reach out my hand and apply pressure to her chin to make her face me. Her eyes are dilated and seem unable to focus.

I take in her features. Those ice blue eyes, full eyelashes, pert little nose, and that luscious mouth. Her thick, raven hair falls to her hips and taunts me. I used to fist that hair while I fucked her from behind. It used to curtain us away from the world when she would lean over me, stroking my face as we made love.

God, I missed her. I knew she was in there somewhere but they had to keep her drugged for everyone's safety.

"I love you, Isabella." I trace my index finger over her thick bottom lip. "I'm trying so hard to keep my promise to you. Unfortunately, our son inherited your madness. Mason makes it so difficult to keep my word to you and protect him."

Shock fills me when her gaze on me sharpens. It must've been Mason's name.

"Do you want me to talk about Mason, sweetheart?" Her eyes bore into mine. I'm wondering if it is our son's name or if her meds are wearing off?

"I just wish you could focus like that when I'm talking about us. Do you remember what it was like between us? I want you back so much, Isabella."

Her eyes glaze back over and I realize the only time she's going to give me her attention is if I talk about Mason. I look around at her room. I had the walls painted pink, pink curtains hung, and a pink comforter put on her bed. Two floral sitting chairs had been arranged in her room and pictures of us were hanging up along with Mason's school portraits over the years.

I spend a fortune on her to be kept in comfort, instead of strapped to a bed in some shitty place, and she can't even gift me with the slightest show of emotion. I let go of her hand and lean back in the chair.

"He kills people, you know. Your dear son, Mason, is a psychopath." I watch in fascination as her eyes jerk back to me and narrow. "He's just like his mother." Deciding I've had enough of this visit. I lean forward and put both hands to her cheeks. "Too bad he'll never know who his real mother is. He'll never know that she was too selfish to be a loving wife and mother."

A single tear slides down her cheek. My tongue traces it's path and I place a kiss to her temple. "Goodbye, my love."

I hear her whimper when I reach the door. My shoulders tense but I refuse to turn around. She chose her path. My heart leads me here once a month but I can't lose myself in her madness. I'd tried to help her control herself all those years ago. It hadn't gotten me anywhere and led down a path to heartache.

Love wasn't always a gift. Mine had been nothing but a fucking curse.

About the Author

Ashley Burton is a new author that decided to never give up her dream of becoming published. She loves escaping into fantasy worlds whether it's through reading or writing her own. Her favorite thing to do is lounge in pajamas while reading a juicy book and sip some whiskey!

She's married to her high school sweetheart and they have two beautiful children. She wants to thank her readers for taking a chance on her and hopes you're not disappointed.

Keep your eyes peeled for book two of the Dark Beast Series...

Coming Soon... Like a Moth to the Flame

54462194R00129

Made in the USA
Columbia, SC
02 April 2019